MANDIE®
AND THE
DARK ALLEY

Mandie® Mysteries

MANDIE®
AND THE
DARK ALLEY

Lois Gladys Leppard

BETHANY HOUSE PUBLISHERS
MINNEAPOLIS, MINNESOTA 55438

Mandie and the Dark Alley
Copyright © 2000
Lois Gladys Leppard

MANDIE® and SNOWBALL® are registered trademarks
of Lois Gladys Leppard.

Cover illustration by Chris Dyrud
Cover design by Eric Walljasper

Published by Bethany House Publishers
A Ministry of Bethany Fellowship International
11400 Hampshire Avenue South
Bloomington, Minnesota 55438
www.bethanyhouse.com

Printed in the United States of America by
Bethany Press International
Bloomington, Minnesota 55438

ISBN 1-55661-674-0

For
Jeanne Mikkelson,

With many thanks to
a dear friend.

About the Author

LOIS GLADYS LEPPARD worked in Federal Intelligence for thirteen years in various countries around the world. She now makes her home in South Carolina.

The stories of her mother's childhood as an orphan in western North Carolina are the basis for many of the incidents incorporated in this series.

Visit with Mandie at *www.Mandie.com*

Contents

"Of making many books
there is no end."

—Ecclesiastes 12:12

Chapter 1 / Forbidden Territory

Mrs. Taft's fancy rig came to a sudden, lurching halt. Mandie and Celia fell against each other as the vehicle swayed and then stopped. The horse added his protest to the crashing sound.

Ben, the driver, called out to the animal, "Whoa there now, whoa!" He jumped down and turned to look up at the girls. "Is y'all all right, missies?" he asked.

Mandie and Celia quickly scrambled down to the street with a helping hand from Ben. The three of them peered through the darkness to survey the damage.

"I'm all right, but what happened, Ben?" Mandie asked, shaking out her long skirts.

"Yes, what happened?" Celia echoed, taking a deep breath.

"Can't rightly tell heah in dis dark place," Ben replied. "Best I ties up dis heah animal and walks y'all on to dat school so's I kin git Uncle Cal to come he'p." He quickly tied the horse's reins to a pole nearby.

"I agree, Ben, because if we're late getting back to school, we'll be in trouble with Miss Prudence," Mandie replied nervously. She removed her hat to rearrange her heavy blond hair, which had loosened from its hairpins in the mishap.

"Is it far to the school, Ben? I don't remember ever being on this street before," Celia asked, looking around in the darkness.

"Dis heah ain't no street. It be a back alley, a shortcut from Miz Taft's house to yo' school. Ain't supposed to be on dis heah place," Ben muttered, more to himself than to the girls. "But I be tryin' to git y'all back on time. Now let's be quick 'bout dis and git on to dat school."

The girls had been to visit Mandie's grandmother, Mrs. Taft, who lived in Asheville not far from the Misses Heathwood's School for Girls, where Mandie and Celia were boarding students. They had stayed for supper, and since it was late Mrs. Taft had sent them back to school in her rig with Ben.

There was no moon. The sky was dark. The uneven cobblestones caused them to stumble now and then as the girls walked along with Ben.

Mandie tried to see where they were and what buildings they were passing. She asked, "Ben, do people live on this street?"

"No, missy, only bidness buildings along heah," Ben answered shortly, hurrying them forward.

Suddenly Mandie stopped and put a hand on

Celia's arm. "Celia, did you hear something?" She tried to see through the darkness in the direction of the sound.

"Yes," Celia agreed. "Like a . . . soft whine."

Ben turned to see what they were doing.

"Oh, it's a puppy!" Mandie exclaimed. "It could be in trouble!"

"No, missy, don't you even think 'bout findin' it," Ben quickly said. "You young ladies shouldn't oughta even be in dis heah alley. It ain't fittin' fo' young ladies to walk in, and I sho' nuff know Miz Taft, she wouldn't be 'llowing it."

"Celia, we'll come back in the daytime and look for it," Mandie murmured as she and Celia continued on their way with Ben.

"No, missy, you don't do dat," Ben said.

"If it's just businesses, why can't we come back? Besides, you drove us down it," Mandie argued.

"And I shouldn'ta oughta done that," Ben replied. "I ain't sure what goes on in dese warehouses. It's dirty and dark, and who knows what be hidin' behind dem walls."

Mandie didn't understand why Ben didn't want them to come back to this alley. Why, she had seen lots of working people who got dirty on their jobs. She was sure there must be some other reason. How could she find out?

"Now, I'se gwine git y'all to dat school safe and sound," Ben said to the girls as the end of the narrow alley came in sight. "We jes' don't hafta tell Miz Taft we came down dat alley, now, do we?"

Mandie looked at him quickly in the darkness and asked, "What about her rig? It's stranded back there in the alley. What if she asks where it broke down?"

Ben scratched his head under his cap and said, "Mebbe I gits de rig fixed real quick, an' Miz Taft, she don't need to know it ever broke down. Jes' let me worry 'bout dat."

Mandie didn't reply but thought about it as they walked on. And lucky for Ben, Uncle Cal, the school caretaker, was coming down the front walkway of the huge mansion that housed the school.

"Y'all walk from Miz Taft's house?" Uncle Cal asked Ben as they approached.

"Not 'zackly," Ben replied. "Rig quit rolling back down de road apiece. Wheel locked up. Mebbe you kin go back wid me and see if we kin git dat rig rolling agin'."

"Sho, I will," Uncle Cal agreed.

The girls bid them good-night and hurried inside the schoolhouse. No one was in the front hallway, and they ran up the stairs to their room. Just as Mandie closed the door, the curfew bell in the backyard began ringing.

"Whew!" she exclaimed, leaning against the door. "We barely made it."

"If we *had* been late for curfew, we probably would have been excused. It wasn't our fault," Celia said, getting her nightclothes out of the big wardrobe.

"You never know about Miss Prudence," Mandie replied, removing her straw hat and tossing it on the bureau. "Now, with Miss Hope, she's always understanding—that is, when her sister, Miss Prudence, is not around. Anyhow, we got back on time, so we won't have to explain to Miss Prudence about the rig breaking down." She pulled her own nightclothes from the wardrobe and began preparing for bed.

"Are we going to keep it a secret—about Ben and the alley and everything?" Celia asked, glancing at Mandie in surprise.

"I don't want Ben to get in trouble," Mandie replied, quickly putting on her nightgown. "Besides, it would create a lot of discussion and maybe more rules. My goodness, you and I are growing up. Fourteen is old enough to be given some freedom. We don't need more supervision and more rules." She flopped into a chair as she talked.

"So, the way I understand it," Celia answered slowly, "you are thinking if everybody knew Ben drove us through that so-called forbidden territory, he would be given strict orders about what routes to go, and we would never be able to make our own decisions about where we want to go. Is that right?" Celia finished as she hung up her dress and came to sit in the other chair in their room.

Mandie grinned at her friend. "That's about right," she agreed. "And remember all the special favors Ben has done for us, like driving us by Mr. Vanderbilt's house so we could see it and going to feed the ducks in that pond out on that country road, and going to stores of our own choice to shop—you know, lots of things like that. We never do anything wrong," she said with another grin. "We just like to make our own choices."

"You're right," Celia agreed. "And your grandmother has been awfully generous with us. She lets Ben drive us in her rig when we need to go some place, and she has done things for us, like the trip to St. Augustine last summer."

"Yes, the trip to St. Augustine," Mandie said enthusiastically. "Grandmother knew I didn't really want to go with her to visit Senator Morton, so I suppose that's why she got all our friends together and brought them down to Florida. Anyway, we did solve the mystery about our clothes being moved around in that wardrobe and that servant who couldn't hear or speak, didn't we?" She laughed at the memories.

"Right," Celia agreed. "Have you decided what you are going to do next summer if Joe stays at college and doesn't come home?"

Mandie frowned and turned to swing her legs over the arm of the big chair. "I don't understand why Joe seems to think he has to study the whole year round instead of going for the usual terms like normal students. He's in such a hurry to get through with school and get into law practice." She paused a moment, then looked at Celia. "But if he doesn't come home for the summer, I'll survive." Mandie smiled.

"Next year will be our last one here at Heathwood's. Mandie, we've got to make a decision about where we are going to college," Celia reminded her.

"I know," Mandie sighed. "I had thought I might like to go where Joe is down in New Orleans, but since I haven't had an opportunity to visit his college, I'm not sure right now."

"That's a long way from home, Mandie," Celia said. "I think we ought to go somewhere near my home in Virginia or yours in North Carolina."

"Well, it might be nice to get away from Grandmother for a while," Mandie replied. "And I'd like to go far enough away from home to have a chance to grow up and become a woman on my own. It's not that far from here to my home in Franklin, but at least my mother doesn't try to keep me under her thumb like Grandmother does. I can imagine what growing up was like for my mother with my grandmother supervising every move she made."

"Then why don't we look at some colleges in Virginia? I wouldn't mind being closer to home," Celia suggested. "Even if we went to a college in Richmond, I wouldn't have to stay at home just because I went to school in the same town where I live. My mother would understand. She wants me to learn to be on my own."

"I just don't know, Celia," Mandie said thoughtfully. "I know I'll have to make a decision soon, and I know that Mother will leave that up to me, no matter how much Grandmother tries to influence the decision."

Celia smiled and said, "I've been wondering how your grandmother will get along with Mollie when Aunt Rebecca brings her for a visit next week."

Mandie also smiled as she replied, "That is Grandmother's idea, to have Mollie stay with her and Hilda for a few days. I'm glad I don't have the job of looking after those two."

"Aunt Rebecca has always gotten along just fine with Mollie since she came to stay with us, but nobody else has any influence on that little Irish orphan," Celia laughed. "So when Aunt Rebecca leaves her with your grandmother, there's no telling what mischief Mollie will get into."

Mandie abruptly changed the subject. "Grandmother has asked me what I would like for a graduation present next year," she said. "I haven't mentioned it to her because she makes such a big to-do about everything. But wouldn't it be nice if you and I could go to Europe again on one of Grandmother's ships—and take Joe, Jonathan, Sallie, and maybe Dimar, and Uncle Ned, of course? Maybe this time we could stay longer and visit all those places we didn't have time for when we went before. What do you think?"

Celia exclaimed, "Oh, Mandie, that would be absolutely wonderful!"

"Do you suppose Senator Morton would go with us next time, like he did the other trip we made?" Mandie asked with a grin.

"Most likely," Celia replied. "One of these days I would not be at all surprised to hear of your grandmother marrying him, would you?"

"I've been expecting it," Mandie agreed. "But I sure would feel sorry for Senator Morton because Grandmother is always the boss." She laughed.

"And who knows, Mandie? We might meet some interesting fellows over there," Celia suggested, sitting up straight in her chair.

"Well, yes, I suppose we could. But that would be a long-distance friendship, and I'd rather have my friends in the United States where I can see them once in a while," Mandie replied.

"We could at least have time for some new friends while we are over there if we stay long enough," Celia said. "Besides, friends move around, you know. Remember, that is how we met

Lily Masterson and her little sister, Violet. They were on the ship with us. And also Jonathan Guyer, and we've stayed in touch with Jonathan."

"Yes, and we ought to look up Lily and see what she has been doing since we saw her," Mandie said.

"They are not all that far away, just down in South Carolina. And you even went to South Carolina once to see Tommy Patton's family in Charleston," Celia said.

"Maybe we could ask Tommy and Robert Rogers to go with us to Europe, too," Mandie said. "They'll be graduating from Mr. Chadwick's School then."

Celia laughed. "Why don't we just take over a whole ship that belongs to your grandmother and take everybody we know?"

Mandie shrugged and said, "That might not be a bad idea. I'll talk to Grandmother about it. It would be like having a reunion before we all go our different ways to college."

Before the girls knew it, the clock on the mantelpiece struck midnight. Tomorrow was a school day, so they rose and stretched.

"Tomorrow is Monday, and that means we have all those extra classes—piano lessons, drama, and the poetry club. So we'd better get some sleep," Mandie said. The two of them pulled down the counterpane and crawled into the big bed.

"You couldn't think of any excuse to bring Snowball back to school with you, could you, Mandie?" Celia asked from her side of the bed.

"You know Miss Prudence doesn't exactly like that white cat of mine. So he's really better off staying with Grandmother," Mandie answered, then added with a laugh, "But who knows when we'll find another rat around here? I'm not sure those workmen closed up all those holes they bored everywhere when they put in the furnace."

"I'll keep my eyes open for one, and then we'll let Miss Prudence know we need Snowball here," Celia said.

"Talking about keeping your eyes open, Celia," Mandie said. "Could you see anything in that dark alley we came through tonight? Could you tell what kind of buildings there were?"

"No, I couldn't see anything distinctly," Celia replied. "In the dark it just looked like a whole lot of old buildings of some kind."

Mandie turned to raise up on her elbow and asked, "Want to go back and see if we can find that puppy?"

"Go back to that alley after Ben said we shouldn't go there?" Celia asked doubtfully.

"What harm could it do in the daytime?" Mandie argued. "I'm curious because Ben was so firm about us not ever going through the place again. Besides, that puppy might need some help. It sounded lonely. And who knows? We might just find another mystery there."

Celia laughed. "Oh, Mandie, you are always looking for a mystery to solve. I'm not sure how we could manage to go back to that alley without someone finding out. You know we aren't supposed to leave the school without supervision and permission. Miss Prudence is really strict about that, too."

"Well, now, when we have a free afternoon

without any classes, we could go for a walk in the front yard here and just keep walking if no one else is around. I don't believe it's very far back to that alley," Mandie said. "And in the daytime the alley wouldn't be dark anyhow."

"That puppy will probably be gone by the time we can get back to look for it," Celia reminded her.

"But it might *not* be gone, either," Mandie argued. "We won't know until we go look. And we have to find the alley first."

"And what would happen to us if we're caught?" Celia wondered.

"Nothing really bad, I don't think," Mandie answered. "Since my grandmother bought this school from Miss Prudence and Miss Hope, those two ladies are not as strict with us as they used to be. And besides, we're getting older, more mature, you know."

"I wouldn't want anything bad on my record since we have only one more year here," Celia said.

"We don't have any misconduct on our record," Mandie declared. She paused for a moment. "But just think of all the escapades we've been able to get away with since we began school here," Mandie said.

"Mandie, we have never been able to get away with anything we weren't supposed to be doing," Celia replied. "We have learned several lessons from things like that. And those lessons should serve us well in our future conduct."

"All right, then, we've never done anything really bad, have we?" Mandie answered. "And I don't intend doing anything bad. It's just that I don't believe going back to that alley would be considered a bad thing. It's really just a case of curiosity, and Grandmother has always said people who are curious learn much faster than others who aren't. And that puppy may still be there if we don't wait too long to go back and look for it."

"All right, all right," Celia agreed with a long sigh. "But let's be sure we don't get into any trouble in that alley."

"We won't," Mandie promised. "We'll be extra careful."

The girls stayed awake for a while longer, planning their return to the dark alley. Mandie felt there was a real mystery connected with it, and she just had to find out what it was and also find the puppy.

Chapter 2 / Trouble!

Schoolwork kept Mandie and Celia busy for a
few days after that. However, Mandie kept remind-
ing Celia that they were going to investigate that
dark alley the first chance they got.

The two girls were sitting in the swing on the
long front porch doing their homework in the warm
October afternoon sunshine. They looked up at the
approach of a horse and buggy.

"Well, hello, Ben," Mandie called as the driver
brought Mrs. Taft's buggy to a halt. Mandie looked
at the vehicle and asked, "Is Grandmother's rig still
broken?"

"Oh no, Uncle Cal and I got dat thing goin' agin
dat night it broke down. Miz Taft, she say take de
buggy, faster dat away," he replied as he came up
the steps. He held out a small white envelope. "Dis
heah fo' you, Missy Manda, from Miz Taft. She say
fo' me to wait fo' you to say whut."

Mandie took the envelope, opened it, and withdrew a small sheet of notepaper. Quickly scanning the short handwritten note, she turned to Celia and said, "Would you believe this? Grandmother is having a little dinner tomorrow night for your aunt Rebecca. She arrived with Mollie today. AND she is inviting TOMMY PATTON and ROBERT ROGERS!" She grinned triumphantly at her friend.

"Really?" Celia excitedly jumped up to read over Mandie's shoulder. "It does say that!"

Mandie looked at Ben and asked, "Did you take invitations to the boys over at Mr. Chadwick's School?"

"I sho did, on de way to heah," Ben said with a big smile. "Now den, I'se got to go. Whut does you want me to tell Miz Taft you said?"

Mandie glanced at Celia. "We don't want to seem too excited, do we?"

"Oh no, that would never do," Celia quickly agreed.

"So we'll treat this as an ordinary invitation to dinner, right?" Mandie said.

"Yes. After all, we do get lots of invitations." Celia nodded knowingly.

Mandie laughed and said, "You know very well that's not true. We only get invitations under the nose of Miss Prudence for right here where she can supervise. And she always watches you and me when the boys come over." Turning to Ben, she said, "Please tell Grandmother we'll be ready and waiting for you to pick us up at four o'clock tomorrow afternoon."

"Yessum, dat I do," Ben replied and turned to leave.

"And, Ben, it'll be dark when we return to the school after dinner," Mandie said, lowering her voice. "Do you think you could drive us down that dark alley again on our way back here?"

"Lawsy mercy, missy! Miz Taft, she wudn't like dat at all." Ben's consternation was clear. "Dat dark alley ain't no place fo' young ladies to go," he said, shaking his head.

"But couldn't we just take the shortcut through there again when we come back to the school? Please, Ben?" Mandie begged. "We won't tell anyone. What harm could it do?"

Ben removed his cap and scratched his head. "Well, I don't know 'bout dat right now. Has to think 'bout it," he said. "I has to go now." He hurried down the front steps.

Mandie and Celia sat back down in the swing as Ben drove away.

"Do you think he'll drive us through that alley tomorrow night?" Mandie asked.

Celia blew out her breath. "Mandie, you're fixing to make trouble for Ben, and we could also be in a lot of trouble if it's found out that we asked Ben to drive through the alley."

"Not we, Celia, just me. I'll take all the blame if we're caught," Mandie answered her. "But I don't see any way that anyone could find out that Ben drove us through there."

"You never know, Mandie," Celia said doubtfully, giving the swing a push to make it move.

"I'll take responsibility for it. I will ask Ben to drive us through there so you won't have to be involved," Mandie told her, looking at the note from her grandmother again. "Do you know how long

Mollie is going to stay with Grandmother?"

"No. It probably depends on how much of Mollie your grandmother can take," Celia said with a laugh.

"I believe Grandmother really loves Mollie. She rescued her from the streets of Belfast, and as you know, Mollie claims her as her own grandmother," Mandie said thoughtfully. Turning to look at her friend, she added, "You know, if we all go to Europe again, we could take Mollie with us. I imagine she would like that, don't you?"

"Oh no, Mandie," Celia quickly responded. "If she gets back in Belfast, we may never be able to get her out again. You know how she is always threatening to just go back to Belfast when things don't go her way."

"It might be a job, but I know my grandmother could get her out and back to the United States," Mandie said. "For one thing, Grandmother has legal custody of her. Remember, the Irish government allowed Grandmother to bring her to the United States because Mollie doesn't have any relatives in Ireland."

"I know, but you remember Mollie is always running away—chasing leprechauns, she says," Celia reminded her.

"Is she still doing that? I mean, at your house, does she run away?" Mandie asked.

"No, not really, because Aunt Rebecca goes with her wherever she wants to go," Celia said.

Mandie's foot stopped the swing. "I have to get this work done so I can go find Miss Prudence and tell her about Grandmother's note. We have to have her permission to leave, you know."

"Right," Celia agreed, bending over her school-book.

Later the girls found Miss Prudence in her office down the hallway from the front door. The lady was bent over papers on her desk and looked up as Mandie and Celia stopped in the doorway.

"Yes?" she asked, peering over her spectacles.

"I have a note here from Grandmother, and we need your permission," Mandie told her, quickly stepping forward and laying the note in front of her.

Without picking it up, Miss Prudence glanced at the note and then looked at Mandie and smiled. "Yes, I know about that," she said. "You see, Mrs. Taft has also invited my sister and me. But since we both can't leave the school at one time, Miss Hope insisted I go."

Mandie frowned, then quickly smiled. "Yes, ma'am," she said. "We told Ben we would be ready by four o'clock tomorrow. Are you driving with us?" she asked.

"No, I have to be able to go and come back on my own schedule. Uncle Cal will drive me in the school rig and wait for me there until I return," Miss Prudence explained. "I am looking forward to spending an evening with your aunt, Celia. She is a fine, upstanding lady. And of course it will be interesting visiting with that little Irish orphan."

"Yes, ma'am," both girls said together.

"You two young ladies plan on being down here and ready to go when Ben arrives," Miss Prudence said, turning back to her papers. Then she quickly added, "And, young ladies, please remember your social graces. I understand Mrs. Taft has invited Thomas Patton and Robert Rogers, also. Remember to conduct yourselves in a ladylike manner. Now, let me get back to work here."

"Thank you, Miss Prudence, I'll remember," Mandie said with a secret smile at her formality.

"Yes, ma'am, Miss Prudence," Celia added as they stepped back into the hallway.

They hurried down the corridor out of sight of Miss Prudence's doorway. "Whew!" Mandie then added, "Shucks! Miss Prudence will be going! Why did Grandmother invite her? She'll put a damper on everything."

"Your grandmother has a huge house. Maybe we can manage to talk to the boys away from Miss Prudence," Celia suggested.

"I hope so. But then there will be Mollie, who will be running all over the place, and we may have to keep up with her," Mandie replied.

As they came to the turn in the hallway that connected with the front corridor, the girls met April Snow. She was hurrying the way they had come. When she saw Mandie and Celia, she suddenly stopped right in front of them.

"Well, well, been to Miss Prudence's office, huh? What have y'all been into this time?" April asked, tossing her long dark hair back over her shoulder.

"Private business, if you must know," Mandie replied, stepping aside to proceed up the hall.

April quickly stepped in front of her again. "Private business—like private trouble you've been in, I'd say," April said with a sneer.

"April, we are not in any trouble," Celia quickly told her.

"And what we just talked about to Miss Prudence is none of your business," Mandie added. "What are you going to see her about? You in trouble again?"

"That's for me to know and you to find out," April said tartly with her most irritating smile.

"Well, get on with it. We have things to do," Mandie said. This time she quickly stepped around the girl and hurried away.

Celia followed. "Mandie, I'm afraid April Snow is on the warpath again," she muttered.

"We'll just ignore her. That's the best way," Mandie declared.

The girls picked up their books where they had left them on the table near the front door and then hurried up the long staircase to their room on the third floor.

"I worry about April Snow, Mandie. You know, she could be a nice person if she wanted to be," Celia said, flopping into one of the big chairs.

Mandie went to sit on the window seat. "There's nothing we can do about it. Maybe one of these days she will realize how she makes other people dislike her," she said. "Anyhow, right now we need to decide what we will wear tomorrow so we can have it all laid out and ready. Our last class will end at three, and that won't leave us much time to get dressed." She got up, went across the room, and opened the huge wardrobe.

Celia followed, and the two stood there, flipping through their hanging clothes.

"Since Grandmother got that banging furnace installed in her house she keeps it pretty warm, so we won't need anything heavy," Mandie remarked.

At that moment the radiator in their room

started hissing and rattling.

"Hear that? The heat is coming up," Celia remarked, looking across the room.

"I wish someone would learn how to run that furnace to keep it just right. It's either freezing cold in here or blazing hot, never in between," Mandie fussed.

"I know," Celia agreed, pulling out a dark green taffeta dress. "I think I'll wear this." She held it up, shaking out the folds.

"In that case, I'll wear my blue taffeta," Mandie said, reaching for the dress.

"You know, this taffeta kinda rattles when we walk," Celia remarked as she shook the skirt of the dress. "We won't be able to sneak up on anyone with this stuff on," she laughed.

Mandie looked at her and smiled. "You mean like Mollie?" she asked.

"Yes, that's the only way to catch up with her sometimes, just sneak up," Celia replied with a big grin.

There was a knock at the door. When Mandie opened it, Aunt Phoebe, the school housekeeper, stood there.

"Oh, come in, Aunt Phoebe," Mandie said, opening the door wide.

Aunt Phoebe frowned as she shook her head and said in a solemn voice, "Miz Prudence, she say fo' you young ladies to come to huh office, right now."

Both girls looked at her in surprise.

"We were just there, Aunt Phoebe. Do you know what she wants?" Mandie asked.

Aunt Phoebe shook her head and replied, "No,

dat I don't know. But de lady was not in a good mood aftuh dat Missy April left huh office."

"April Snow!" Mandie exclaimed as she and Celia looked at each other. "I thought April was up to something."

"Oh, Mandie, she is probably trying to make trouble for us," Celia said.

Aunt Phoebe said, "Best you be gittin' on dere and face de music." She went on back down the hallway.

"What could April Snow have said to Miss Prudence to make her call us down there like that?" Mandie moaned.

"Well, come on, Mandie. We'd better not keep the lady waiting," Celia said, starting for the door.

"Why does April Snow always have to be causing trouble? I don't know of anything that we've done wrong that she could be telling Miss Prudence, do you?" Mandie asked as they went down the long hallway.

"No, I can't think of a thing," Celia replied.

"You know, April Snow has been known to make things up," Mandie reminded her.

They came to the top of the steps and stopped.

"Mandie, she is always eavesdropping on people and telling everything she hears," Celia said.

"Eavesdropping? I haven't seen her around any place we've been lately, so what could she have heard that we said?" Mandie wondered.

"I haven't seen her, either, but she's like a ghost the way she appears and disappears so suddenly in unexpected places," Celia said.

"Well, come on, we'll soon know," Mandie said, starting down the stairs.

The girls were reluctant to face whatever Miss Prudence might have waiting for them. As they slowly entered the hallway to Miss Prudence's office, they were surprised to see her standing outside the doorway.

"Get a move on, young ladies," Miss Prudence called to them. "I have work to do."

The girls hurried on down to meet her. They followed Miss Prudence into her office, where the lady sat down behind her desk. She did not invite the girls to sit. They stood nervously before her desk.

Mandie wanted to get this over with. "We're here, Miss Prudence. Aunt Phoebe said you wanted to see us," she said, clearing her throat.

Miss Prudence looked sharply at her and then at Celia. "I know very well you are here," she said. Pausing for a moment, she then said, "I want an explanation from you two."

The girls didn't reply but silently watched the lady.

"Do you hear me?" the lady asked.

"Yes, ma'am," Mandie and Celia both answered.

"Well then, speak when you are spoken to," Miss Prudence said.

"Yes, ma'am," the girls both replied again.

"Now, it has been brought to my attention that you two young ladies have asked Ben to drive you through some alley somewhere, and I want to know what that is all about," Miss Prudence demanded.

Mandie's heartbeat quickened as she tried to

think of an explanation. Though they had not seen her, evidently April had been eavesdropping on their conversation with Ben.

"It's just a . . . a shortcut out . . . to my grandmother's house," Mandie haltingly explained.

"What shortcut? Where is this alley?" Miss Prudence asked.

Mandie and Celia looked at each other.

"I don't know, Miss Prudence," Mandie replied.

"We don't know," Celia repeated.

"I asked a question and I want a sensible answer," Miss Prudence announced. "Young ladies attending this school do not venture forth into the alleyways of Asheville for any reason whatsoever, as you two are well aware. Now, I want to know where this alley is, and how did you two learn of it?"

Mandie looked at Celia. Then she said, "The truth is, Miss Prudence, we really don't know where the alley is. It's just that when Ben was bringing us back to school from Grandmother's house Sunday night, her rig broke down in a dark street somewhere and Ben said it was not a good place to be, so we didn't tell anyone because we didn't want Ben to get in trouble."

"Is your grandmother aware of this?" Miss Prudence asked.

"I don't suppose so, Miss Prudence," Mandie said. "We haven't seen Grandmother since then, and I don't know whether Ben told her or not."

"Now, furthermore, I understand you were asking Ben to drive you back through that alley after you leave your grandmother's house tomorrow night," Miss Prudence said, watching the girls closely.

Mandie felt her face grow hot. April had overheard all this and was trying to make trouble over it. She took a deep breath and said, "Miss Prudence, we—or I should say I, because Celia did not ask or agree—I just wanted to see where the alley is. We couldn't tell much that night when the rig broke down. It was too dark—"

"You want to know where this alley is? For what reason? Why should you want to know where an alleyway is?" Miss Prudence interrupted, her tone stern.

"Well, for one thing, so we would know not to go back that way again," Mandie replied somewhat lamely. She silently argued with herself that was part of the reason anyhow.

"You are supposed to be chaperoned any time you leave this school," Miss Prudence reminded her. "That is not for you to decide. Ben knows better than to take anyone down those dark alleyways. I will have to speak to your grandmother about this. You may go now."

"Yes, ma'am, thank you, Miss Prudence," Mandie managed to mumble as she and Celia left the office.

Rushing down the hallway to the front corridor, Mandie came to a halt in the foyer. She angrily said, "I'll get even with April Snow. You just wait and see. She not only got us in trouble, she has also made trouble for Ben. It wasn't his fault that the rig broke down."

"I know, Mandie, but there is nothing we can do about it now," Celia soothed. "Come on. Let's go back up to our room till it's time to eat.'' She started toward the wide staircase.

"Yes, there is something I can do, and believe me, I will think up something to do to April Snow for this,'' Mandie fumed as she followed Celia up the stairs.

"That would just make matters worse,'' Celia reminded her.

"Not exactly. If I can figure out something that will make trouble for her . . .'' Mandie muttered. That April Snow was forever causing trouble, poking into things that didn't even concern her. Well, Mandie would poke into April Snow's affairs and find something to make trouble for her. Mandie seethed inwardly as she slammed their door shut.

Chapter 3 / Did Miss Prudence Tell?

The excitement of going to Mrs. Taft's dinner party was dulled by the trouble caused by April Snow.

"I almost wish we weren't going," Mandie said, blowing through her teeth in frustration as she and Celia sat in the alcove near the front door, waiting for Ben to pick them up.

"Why, Mandie? Remember, Tommy and Robert will be there," Celia reminded her, straightening the folds of her taffeta dress and then pushing back her auburn curls.

"That's the problem," Mandie moaned as she moved restlessly. "It might turn out to be really embarrassing if they overhear Miss Prudence telling my grandmother about the alley."

"But, Mandie, it would probably be exciting to them to hear that we've been down a dark alley late at night and plan to go back," Celia argued.

"They are boys, and boys love adventurous doings like that."

"I'm afraid they would have the same opinion that Miss Prudence did, that young ladies don't go in such places," Mandie said.

Celia looked out the window and stood. "Well, here's Ben," she said, quickly putting on her cloak.

Mandie picked up her cloak from a chair and slipped into it, pulling the hood over her long blond hair. She looked at Celia and said, "I suppose it's only fair to warn Ben that Miss Prudence is about to tell all."

"Yes, I would," Celia agreed.

The late-afternoon temperature was dropping. The girls hurried down the front steps.

"Howdy, missies," Ben greeted them as he stood waiting by the rig.

The girls quickly stepped into the vehicle, and Ben climbed up on the driver's seat and shook the reins.

"Oh, Ben, I'm afraid we have some bad news." Mandie leaned forward as the rig rolled down the street.

"Bad news? Whut bad news dat?" Ben asked, glancing back from his seat.

"I'm sorry to say it's really bad news, Ben, for you and for us—or me, I should say. And I was the one who caused it," Mandie replied, trying to explain.

"Ah, now, missy, you don't never cause bad news. You go round fixin' up bad news," Ben assured her as he guided the vehicle down the street.

"Ben, you know who that April Snow is at our school, don't you?" Mandie asked.

"Yeh, now, dat's de troublemaker fo' sho'," he said.

"Well, she has caused some trouble for us. You see, when I was asking you if you would drive us back through that dark alley tonight after we leave Grandmother's house, she was eavesdropping and she went straight and told Miss Prudence, and Miss Prudence called us into her office and said she is going to tell my grandmother tonight. My grandmother invited her to come for dinner tonight, too." Mandie, exasperated, finished her explanation in a rush.

Ben scratched his head under his cap. "Well now, missy, we jes' won't go back down dat alley. Den ain't nuthin' to tell."

"But, Ben, I had to explain to Miss Prudence how we knew about the alley. I had to tell her the rig broke down when we took a shortcut back to the school that night," Mandie groaned. "I'm sorry."

"Wudn't no harm done, so Miz Taft, she ain't gwine git upset 'bout dat. All she do will be say don't go back dat way agin, and we sho' ain't gwine back dat way agin," Ben replied, glancing back at Mandie with a big smile. "Don't let it worry you none, missy."

"I'm just dreading this visit at my grandmother's, and I hope we don't have to stay late," Mandie said, sitting back in her seat.

The girls were the first to arrive, and Mrs. Taft was directing Ella, her maid, as to what dishes and linens to use that night. Annie, the bedroom maid, had let them in the front door, and after removing their wraps they found Mrs. Taft in the dining room.

"Use the small silver set for the coffee, Ella. Mrs. Manning has asked to borrow the large one for a dinner she is giving for her church, and if we don't use it tonight you won't have to polish it up for her," Mrs. Taft was saying to Ella, who was removing dishes from the china closet. She turned when she saw the girls enter the room.

"Where is everybody, Grandmother? Aunt Rebecca and Mollie and Hilda?" Mandie asked.

Mrs. Taft smiled at her granddaughter and Celia. "Celia's aunt Rebecca is reading to them in the back parlor and trying to keep them out of mischief while I get everything set up. So please don't disturb them right now."

"I won't," Mandie agreed, smiling. She knew how active Mollie was.

Mrs. Taft turned back to the maid and said, "Ella, while you're in the cabinet, get down that large set and set it on the buffet so it'll be handy when Mrs. Manning comes after it."

"Yessum," Ella replied, climbing up on a stool to reach the top shelf of the glass-doored china cabinet.

Mandie hurried across the room and held up her arms. "I'll help you, Ella. Just give me a piece at a time and I'll set it down for you," she said.

"Thank you, Missy Manda," Ella answered warmly. "That be a big help." She carefully passed each part of the silver down, and Mandie carefully placed them on the buffet. She stepped back to admire the fancy coffeepot, sugar bowl, and cream pitcher she had set on the matching silver tray. Each piece had been polished to shine like a looking glass.

Annie came to the doorway and announced, "More company knockin' at de door."

"Well, go let them in," Mrs. Taft instructed. Turning to the girls she said, "You two go receive them for me and I'll be with y'all shortly. Take them to the front parlor."

"Yes, ma'am," Mandie replied eagerly, imagining the new arrivals to be Tommy Patton and Robert Rogers. She winked at Celia, and they followed Annie down the hallway and went on into the parlor while the maid continued to the front door.

"It's probably Tommy and Robert," Mandie whispered to Celia as they quickly sat down on a settee near the fireplace.

But then the next minute Mandie could hear Annie saying, "Yes, ma'am, right dis way, please, ma'am. I take yo' wraps and put dem right heah."

Mandie looked at Celia and made a face. "Must be Miss Prudence," she whispered, and Celia nodded in agreement.

In a moment the schoolmistress appeared at the doorway to the parlor. Mandie and Celia both stood up. "Come right in, Miss Prudence. My grandmother said she would be with us shortly. Have a seat, please, ma'am," Mandie said, nodding toward a seat near the warmth of the fireplace.

"Thank you, Amanda, Celia," Miss Prudence replied as she sat down in the large chair. She pulled the cover back on the watch she wore on a chain around her neck. "I suppose I am a little early."

"And we were earlier than you. Or maybe Grandmother is just running late," Mandie remarked as she and Celia sat back down.

"Yes, I apologize, Miss Prudence. I am running a little late," Mrs. Taft said, hurrying into the room. "Those two children are a handful to keep up with." She went to sit opposite Miss Prudence. Turning back to Celia, she said, "Celia, dear, would you please go let your aunt Rebecca know Miss Prudence has arrived?"

"Yes, ma'am," Celia replied.

As Celia left the room, Mandie quickly stood and followed her.

"I'll go with her," Mandie explained to the two ladies by the fireplace.

When Celia opened the door, Aunt Rebecca was sitting on the settee by the window, with Mollie on one side of her and Hilda on the other. She was reading to the girls from a book in her lap.

Mollie instantly jumped down from the settee and ran to Mandie.

"Mandie, does my grandmother have leprechauns in this house? Does she? Do you know?" Mollie asked insistently. "Does she?"

Mandie bent down to embrace the small child. "Of course not, Mollie," she replied. "Remember, I told you there are no such things as leprechauns."

"Oh, but you said there are no leprechauns in the house where you live," Mollie replied, shaking her red curls. "Might there be leprechauns in this house then, my grandmother's house? Do you know? Do you?" She pulled at Mandie's skirt as Mandie stood.

"Mollie, don't you remember I told you we just don't have leprechauns in the United States," Mandie said with a smile.

"Mrs. Taft sent us to tell you that Miss Prudence

has arrived and they are in the front parlor," Celia told her aunt.

"Thank you, dear," Aunt Rebecca said, standing up and placing the book on a table nearby. She turned to look at Mollie. "Now, Mollie, we must act like a grown-up lady tonight, remember? Special guests are coming to join us, and we want them to see what a nice little girl you are."

Mollie frowned and crossed her feet as she stood there. "Will it be all right if I be asking them whether they be having leprechauns at their house maybe?"

"We will see," Aunt Rebecca answered, shaking her head with a smile. She left the room with Mollie following closely behind her.

Mandie turned to Hilda, who was still sitting on the settee. "Hilda, do you want to come into the parlor with us? Everyone is going in there," she explained.

Hilda was always quiet and shy. Mandie and Celia had found her hiding in the attic of their schoolhouse a long time ago, and Mrs. Taft had given her a home. She did not talk, and everyone wondered whether she was able to speak or not. Then at one time a while ago, she had seemed to understand Cherokee when Mandie's father's old friend Uncle Ned had been speaking. Her parents had kept her shut up in a room and didn't know what to do with her. They were greatly relieved when Mrs. Taft took charge of her.

Mandie watched to see what Hilda would do. The girl pushed back her long dark hair and stood up. The she suddenly ran out of the room and disappeared down the hallway in the opposite direction of the parlor.

"Oh well," Mandie said. "I suppose she will come back and join us when she gets ready."

As Celia started to go down the hallway toward the parlor, Mandie laid a hand on her arm to stop her. In a low voice she asked, "Do you suppose Miss Prudence has told Grandmother about the alley yet?"

"Maybe," Celia whispered.

There was a sound of voices in the front hallway, and Mandie quickly said, "Must be Tommy and Robert." She grinned at her friend as the two of them hurried on down the corridor.

Tall, handsome Thomas Patton had just hung up his coat and hat when he looked over and saw Mandie. Robert Rogers was right behind him, and he smiled shyly at Celia.

"It was nice of your grandmother to ask us over tonight," Tommy said after he had greeted Mandie.

"Let's let her know y'all are here," Mandie said, leading the way to the parlor. Mrs. Taft looked up when they entered the room. "Grandmother, here is Tommy Patton and also Robert Rogers."

Everyone exchanged greetings, and the young people sat down at one side of the room. Mollie, who had been sitting on a stool by Aunt Rebecca, immediately jumped up and ran over to join them, pulling a footstool over by Tommy.

"Do you be having leprechauns at your house?" the little girl asked.

Tommy smiled. "No, we have no leprechauns. But, come to think of it, we did have a ghost at our house one time." He grinned at Mandie.

"There was a ghost? Will the ghost come back again?" Mollie asked, frowning as she tossed back her red curls. "Will it?"

Mandie was becoming irritated with all these questions from Mollie. "Mollie, let's not talk about leprechauns and ghosts anymore. Tommy and I would like to talk about something else," she told the little girl.

"All right then, you talk, I listen," Mollie replied and sat straight up on the stool to look from Mandie to Tommy.

Tommy laughed and asked Mandie, "Where is her playmate? You said Hilda was here."

"I don't know where Hilda went. She was in the back parlor when we went to get Aunt Rebecca."

Mollie quickly reached over to pull on Mandie's skirt. "I be knowing where Hilda went," she said. "You want Hilda to come in here? I go get her."

Before anyone could reply, Mollie jumped up and ran out of the parlor.

"Goodness knows where she will go, but at least there are two maids in the house. So maybe they'll look out for her," Mandie said with a big sigh of relief.

"But this house is so big she might not be seen," Celia remarked. "I imagine she knows where Hilda went and will stay with her. Since Mollie came to live at our house, Aunt Rebecca said she has been lonely with no other child around. So I imagine Mollie is glad to have Hilda."

Tommy Patton cleared his throat, grinned at Mandie, and glanced at Celia. "Say, that was quite a daring escapade you girls were on the other night, according to what I've heard," Tommy said teasingly.

Mandie felt her face turn red. "What escapade, Tommy Patton?"

"Going through that dark alley and your grand-mother's rig breaking down in the middle of it," Tommy explained with a grin.

"It's the talk of our school right now," Robert added, glancing at Celia.

"It wasn't our fault," Celia quickly said.

"How did y'all know about that?" Mandie aked.

"We were going down Main Street in our school's rig that night when we saw Uncle Cal and Ben walking down the street. So we stopped and offered them a ride," Tommy said, still grinning. "Ben directed us to the alley where Mrs. Taft's rig was sitting. They said they could fix it, so we didn't stay to help because we would have been late for our curfew. Some adventure."

Celia grinned at Mandie and said, "See, I told you so."

Mandie lowered her voice and said, "I don't think Grandmother knows about that yet, but Miss Prudence said she is going to tell her and we may get in trouble."

"What for? It wasn't your fault," Robert put in.

"No, it wasn't, but you know how Miss Prudence is. From the way she talked, she seemed to think we should have kept Ben from going through there," Mandie said.

"But we were only taking a shortcut to school in order to get back before the curfew bell. And Mrs. Taft herself kept us here that late, so I don't think Mrs. Taft will be too upset about it," Celia said.

Mandie looked at Celia and said, "You're right. I hadn't thought about that. It was my grandmother who almost made us late in getting back to school. We were having a conversation about Mollie's visit here, and no one noticed the time until Grandmother suddenly looked at the clock and rushed us off back to school."

"It's good you girls had Ben with you, because I understand that is a deserted warehouse area, and all kinds of tramps hang out there," Tommy said to the girls. "Even the boys at our school are forbidden to go there."

"We wouldn't have been there without Ben because he was the one who knew the shortcut through there," Mandie said. "What is in those warehouses in that alley? Ben only said it was businesses of some kind."

Robert laughed and said, "I doubt there's much business going on down that alley. It's just old dilapidated warehouses that ought to be torn down."

"And how do you know that?" Celia asked teasingly.

"Well, I don't know anything about it for sure, just what I've heard and what Mr. Chadwick said when he put it off limits for our school," Robert explained.

"If the place is isolated and no one lives or works there, I wonder what a puppy was doing in there. I know I heard a puppy whine while we were standing on the street after the rig broke down," Mandie said.

"It was probably a stray dog of some kind," Tommy said.

"It sounded like a small puppy, and I've been wanting to go back and see about it," Mandie said.

"Oh no, I wouldn't go back in there if I were you. There might be bums hanging around those old buildings," Tommy quickly told her.

"It would be all right to go there in the daytime to look for that puppy, wouldn't it?" Mandie asked.

"No, no, bums don't just pack up and leave wherever they are staying when it gets daylight. No, I'd say stay away from there," Tommy replied.

Later, as everyone sat around the dining table, Mandie thought about the conversation with Tommy. Should she attempt to go back in that alley and look for the puppy?

Mollie had come back to the parlor holding Hilda by the hand, practically dragging the girl along with her, just as Mrs. Taft led the group to the dining room for the evening meal. Aunt Rebecca had immediately taken charge and placed the two girls on either side of her at the table, to Mandie's relief. She and Celia wanted a chance to talk to Tommy and Robert without interruptions from Mollie.

And while Mandie talked with Tommy, she tried to watch her grandmother and Miss Prudence to figure out whether the schoolmistress had told Mrs. Taft about their shortcut through the alley. The adults were involved in their own conversation, and Mollie and Hilda were interested in their food.

Then Mandie realized the boys knew where the alley was, and if she could find out the location from them, then she and Celia wouldn't have to go all over town looking for it. That is, if they decided to take a chance and go back.

"This alley isn't really very far from our school, is it?" Mandie asked Tommy as she laid down her fork.

"Only a few blocks from Main Street, actually. Go north on King Street and you run right into it," Tommy explained. "Mr. Chadwick had made it clear to us about the exact location so we couldn't say we wandered down there by mistake."

"And I don't suppose you fellows ever have done that?" Mandie asked with a grin.

Tommy laughed and said, "Keep this secret, but that is the *first* thing we did. Most of the boys slipped off down there just to see why it was off limits. But, believe me, it is an awfully trashy place. I wouldn't recommend that you girls go check it out."

Mandie still couldn't understand why everyone thought the alley was dangerous in the daytime, if it was that close to Main Street. Back in her hometown of Franklin, everyone walked down any street any time of the day without thinking about danger.

She determined she would go back and check on that puppy as soon as she got a chance. She hoped it would still be there.

When everyone said good-night later, and Ben drove the girls back to their school, there was no mention of the alley from Mandie's grandmother. So she decided that Miss Prudence hadn't told her about it. Why, she could not figure out, because Miss Prudence went strictly by the rules.

Anyhow, the girls breathed a sigh of relief when they got back in their room. Maybe nothing more would be said about the alley.

Chapter 4 / Dangerous Errand

The next morning Mandie and Celia were almost late for breakfast. Mandie had decided to wear a new navy woolen dress with twenty-two buttons down the front. Trying to hurry, Mandie's fingers fumbled as she tried to button each one.

"Oh, shucks, why did Grandmother have so many buttons put on this dress?" she exclaimed in frustration, halfway up the row.

"You shouldn't criticize a present, Mandie. Just think how much your grandmother must have paid to have the dress made," Celia scolded mildly as she brushed her long auburn curls. "Besides, I think those little pearl buttons are just beautiful."

"Beautiful, but lots of trouble," Mandie said, straightening up with a sigh. "Finally I got to the end. Now, where is my locket?" She quickly went to her jewelry box on the bureau and took out her most treasured possession, a locket with her father's picture inside. She fastened the chain around her neck. "Guess I'm ready now."

"Let's go," Celia said, opening the door to the hallway.

The two girls hurried down the long staircase from their room on the third floor of the schoolhouse.

"Oh, the line is moving," Mandie said as she looked over the banister at the other pupils heading toward the dining room.

Just as the two got to the bottom step, Miss Hope came hurrying around the corner of the hallway and motioned to them.

Mandie glanced at the end of the line disappearing into the dining room. Why was Miss Hope making them late for breakfast? Miss Prudence didn't condone tardiness in anything. This was her week to preside at the first sitting for breakfast, and she might just close them out.

"Amanda, Celia," Miss Hope said breathlessly, catching up with them. "I wonder if you two young ladies would mind doing a big favor for me this afternoon."

"I would be glad to, Miss Hope," Mandie said, smiling. She glanced nervously toward the dining room door, which was still open.

"Yes, ma'am," Celia said. "Anything you say, Miss Hope."

"My sister, Miss Prudence, has come down with a cold this morning and is confined to her room for the day, so I cannot leave the school myself," Miss Hope explained. "I need to pick up some sheet music from Heyward's downtown, and I was wondering if you two would mind getting it for me. I could send Uncle Cal, but you see, he wouldn't be able to read the list."

"Oh, we would be glad to, Miss Hope," Mandie said with another smile. Relieved, she glanced at Celia, realizing Miss Prudence would not be waiting in the dining room to reprimand them for being late. "Just tell us what you need and we'll get it for you."

"Thank you, Amanda," Miss Hope replied, also smiling, as she moved on toward the dining room door. "Come. I have to sit through two breakfasts this morning since my sister is not able to preside over her group. Now, I'll send Uncle Cal with you, and I'll get a list made up before classes are out today. I appreciate your help, young ladies."

Both girls replied, "Thank you, Miss Hope." They followed Miss Hope into the dining room.

When classes were over at three that afternoon, the girls found Miss Hope waiting for them in the hallway.

"Please hurry and get your wraps now. It will be chilly before you get back. And, remember, the days are getting shorter, too," Miss Hope told them. "Uncle Cal is waiting in the rig in the front driveway. Be sure you go straight to the store and back, under the supervision of Uncle Cal at all times. Understood?"

"Yes, ma'am," both girls replied.

"Here is the list. If you have any problems with it, just talk to Mr. Heyward himself. He will know what I want," the headmistress explained, handing a folded sheet of paper to Mandie.

"Yes, ma'am," Mandie said, taking the paper.

"Now, I have to get back to the office to other

duties. When you return, bring the music sheets straight to me there,'' Miss Hope said, turning away.

The girls hurried upstairs, grabbed their hooded cloaks, and rushed down to where Uncle Cal was waiting. Uncle Cal had been at the school for many years. He was Aunt Phoebe's husband, and the couple had their own little house on the grounds behind the main building.

"You know where we are going, don't you, Uncle Cal?'' Mandie asked as she and Celia stepped up into the rig.

"Dat I does,'' Uncle Cal said with a smile from the front seat. He glanced back as the girls sat down and then shook the reins. The horse trotted down the driveway.

Mandie glanced at the paper Miss Hope had given her. "Since I am not sure what this all means, I'll just give it to Mr. Heyward. I suppose we can just wait while he gets things together,'' she said.

Celia looked at the list Mandie was holding. "Looks like some really old classical music,'' she remarked. "I suppose we will be going into more complicated music lessons soon.''

"That's what I was thinking,'' Mandie agreed. "Unless this order is just for Miss Hope herself, or maybe for Miss Prudence.''

"Look, Mandie. We're going down Main Street,'' Celia pointed toward a sign. "Is Mr. Heyward's store on Main Street?''

"Yes. Miss Hope has written here that Mr. Heyward's store is on Main Street,'' Mandie replied, scanning the sheet of paper. She looked around and suddenly caught her breath. "And there's King

Street that we just crossed."

Uncle Cal slowed the rig and pulled into a space in front of a tall, slender building bearing the name "Heyward's" over the doorway.

"I waits right heah whilst you young ladies goes inside and does de bidness fo' Miz Hope," Uncle Cal told them as he stepped down from the rig to help the girls out.

"This is a long list, Uncle Cal. I don't know how long it will take," Mandie told him, holding up the sheet of paper as she and Celia headed for the front door.

"I be heah," the old man replied, hooking the reins over the hitching post.

Mandie and Celia stepped inside the store and looked around. A huge piano stood near the front door. On the other side was a glass showcase containing violins. Toward the back were racks of sheet music, pamphlets, and instruction books.

"This is a big store," Mandie commented as they slowly walked on through. No one seemed to be around. She turned back to Celia. "I wonder where we can find Mr. Heyward."

Before Celia could reply, a tall elderly man with thick gray hair and spectacles perched on his long nose appeared from the side. "I'm right here, young ladies," he greeted them. "Now, what can I do for you today?"

"Oh, Mr. Heyward, Miss Hope sent us with a list that she needs," Mandie told him, stopping to let him catch up with them in the middle aisle. She held out the sheet of paper.

"Miss Hope, now, there's one nice lady," Mr. Heyward said with a smile, taking the paper and peering through his glasses at it. "Seems she has quite a list here."

"Yes, sir, that's what we thought, too. If you don't mind gathering up all those things for her, we'll just look around as we wait," Mandie replied.

"Yes, ma'am, be glad to. Y'all just make yourselves at home now. This will take a few minutes," he said, looking at the list as he disappeared behind shelves of merchandise.

Mandie and Celia roamed the store, looking at everything, and then Mandie happened to notice there was another entrance into the store from the street behind the building. She stopped to look out through the glass door. From what she could see, the neighborhood back there seemed to be old and run-down.

Celia came to her side. "Looks like alleys back there to me," she remarked.

"Alleys!" Mandie exclaimed. "You are right. And we crossed King Street, remember, the one that Tommy and Robert mentioned. Let's go take a look while Mr. Heyward gets the order together." She pushed on the door.

"Mandie, wait," Celia protested, but she followed Mandie outside. "I don't think we ought to go out here by ourselves. Besides, Uncle Cal is waiting for us."

"Come on. It won't take but a few minutes to walk down this street and back. Come on," Mandie urged. She began rapidly walking toward the next alleyway.

Celia skipped and caught up with her. "Oh, Mandie, I don't really feel right about this. We could get in trouble," she reminded her friend. "And it could be dangerous."

"In the daytime? Who's going to bother us in the daytime?" Mandie replied, hurrying across the side street.

"How will we know the alley when we see it? It was dark that night, remember?" Celia asked, panting along behind Mandie.

"I'll know it," Mandie declared, leading the way across several other streets that looked more and more like alleys. She kept looking down the side streets. Now and then she saw someone walking, but the cobblestone corridor through the maze of buildings was mostly isolated.

Celia stayed close by her side. "Mandie, don't you think we've looked enough and we ought to go back now?" she asked timidly.

"In a minute, Celia. I just want to see a little more," Mandie replied without slowing down.

Then they came to an alley that ran across the street they were on. It was narrow, hardly wide enough for a rig to pass through, with old dilapidated buildings along each side. Mandie quickly stopped.

"This is it!" she declared excitedly, turning to enter the alley. "There are the old buildings we couldn't see very well at night, and the cobblestones are rough and lopsided in places, and all those straggly trees growing in between everything." She quickly walked into the passageway.

Celia followed on her heels. "Well, now we've found it, so let's go back, Mandie," she begged.

"I wonder exactly where the rig broke down," Mandie murmured. "It was near there that I thought

I heard the puppy whining, remember?" She stopped to look around and listen.

"I don't hear it now," Celia whispered, huddling close to Mandie's side.

"I don't, either, but look! There's a man leaning on the side of a building down there. Let's just ask him if he has seen a puppy around here," Mandie said, moving forward.

"Mandie!" Celia groaned in protest.

As they approached, Mandie saw the man was poorly dressed—holes in the knees of his dirty pants, and his shirt, too small for him, was gaping at the buttons. He had a cap pulled down to shade his eyes as he watched them come closer.

Mandie stopped within ten feet of the man and asked, "Mister, have you seen a puppy around here? We heard one crying the other night and came back to look for it," she explained.

The man grunted something unintelligible and suddenly turned to push aside a board in the wall of the building behind him. He stepped inside, then turned to peep out through the cracks.

Mandie, slightly afraid, controlled her voice as she asked, "Well, have you seen a lost puppy?"

The man suddenly spat tobacco juice through the crack, barely missing the girls, and hissed, "Git."

Mandie and Celia almost knocked each other down as they turned to flee back the way they had come. Mandie ran into a low branch of one of the trees, and it caught the fabric on the open collar of her cloak.

"Oh, shucks!" she cried, thoroughly frightened now. She managed to jerk her collar free and continued to run up the street.

Finally within sight of the Heyward store, they stopped to look back.

"That man must have been one of those bums Tommy and Robert said are known to hang out in that street," Mandie said, catching her breath and brushing at her skirts.

"Yes, come on, Mandie. Let's get back inside the store before he comes after us," Celia gasped out, rushing toward the back door.

"I don't think he'll follow us here," Mandie said as they entered Heyward's store.

Mandie looked around and didn't see anyone. She decided Mr. Heyward must still be gathering up the order.

"Let's sit down, Mandie, before my legs collapse," Celia said in a shaky voice, walking toward a long bench in the middle aisle.

As soon as the girls sat down, Mr. Heyward came back into the store from a side door, his arms full of parcels.

"Sorry to keep you young ladies waiting so long, but I had to go through some stock to find everything Miss Hope wanted. Now, where is your driver? I'll give these to him," Mr. Heyward explained, walking toward the front door to look outside.

Out on the sidewalk, Uncle Cal had seen Mr. Heyward and came to the door to accept the packages.

"Please tell Miss Hope I appreciate her order very much, and I hope you come back to visit," Mr. Heyward said to the girls.

"Thank you, sir," Mandie replied, slipping through the doorway.

"Yes, thank you, sir," Celia added, quickly following.

Uncle Cal helped the girls up the steps of the rig, then jumped onto his seat up front, and they were on their way back to school.

"Did you get tired waiting for us, Uncle Cal?" Mandie asked, hoping to find out whether he might have wandered around and seen them go out the back door.

Uncle Cal glanced back. "No, ma'am, missy, dat was purty quick like. When I brings Miz Hope to dis store, she stay long time, play dat big piano, talk to de Mistuh Heyward, and look at jes' 'bout ev'rything in de store, she do."

Mandie smiled and said, "Well, I'm glad you didn't mind waiting for us." She turned to Celia and said under her breath, "Do you think Miss Hope might be interested in Mr. Heyward?" She grinned at her friend.

Celia grinned back. "Could be," she agreed.

When they returned to the school, Uncle Cal took the packages to the office, and the girls rushed upstairs to their room. It was getting late and would soon be time for supper. And the girls didn't want to be late for that meal. Miss Prudence might have recovered and be presiding at the table.

"Oh, that was exciting, wasn't it?" Mandie said triumphantly as she removed her cloak and hung it up in the wardrobe.

"No, that was dangerous, Mandie," Celia argued, coming to hang her cloak alongside Mandie's. "I hope you don't plan on going back there, ever."

"But I've got to go back to look for the puppy," Mandie told her, going over to the bureau and picking up her brush to straighten her blond hair.

Celia came to join her, brushing her own auburn curls and preparing to tie her hair back with a ribbon. Suddenly she turned to look carefully at Mandie. "Where is your locket, Mandie?" she asked.

Mandie quickly felt for the locket as she gazed into the mirror. "Oh, Celia, I've lost it!" she cried, examining the collar of her dress. "What will I do? I *have* to go back now. You know it has the only picture of my father in it that I have. Oh, goodness!" Tears came into her blue eyes.

"Mandie, I understand, I understand," Celia said, trying to comfort her. "And I'll even go back with you to look for it. This is much more important than a puppy."

"You will? Oh, thank you, Celia!" Mandie replied, turning to give Celia a quick hug. "Thank you."

"We won't be able to go back until after supper, and it's going to be awfully dark then," Celia noted nervously.

"We'll take a lantern, that's what we'll do," Mandie decided.

"But how are we going to get permission to go back to that alley?" Celia asked.

"We won't get permission because it would not be granted. So we'll just wait until everyone goes to their rooms after supper and then we'll slip out," Mandie replied.

Suddenly there was a loud meow from under the big bed. Mandie rushed over to kneel on the floor.

"Snowball!" she cried excitedly as she held up the edge of the counterpane. "Come out from under there. How did you get here? Celia, it's Snowball. Where did he come from?"

Celia joined her as the white cat slowly made its way out from under the bed. Mandie snatched him up and squeezed him tight, causing him to loudly protest.

"I wonder how he got here," Mandie said again, sitting on the floor with the cat in her lap. She certainly was happy to see her cat but could not figure out how he got to their room. Then the bell in the backyard announced supper. The girls made sure Snowball was shut up in the room and went down to the dining room.

Miss Hope met them in the front hallway. "I appreciate your running that errand for me, young ladies," she told them as they walked toward the dining room.

"You are welcome," Mandie quickly said. "But, Miss Hope, how did Snowball get in my room? I mean, he was at Grandmother's house."

Miss Hope smiled and said, "My sister thought she heard a mouse while she has been staying in her room all day, so I took it on myself to send for your cat. I will inform my sister after supper that he is here."

"Oh, thank you, Miss Hope." Mandie beamed. Then she said mischievously, "I'm so glad Miss Prudence thought she heard a mouse." All three laughed.

As soon as the evening meal was over, the girls went back to their room with food for Snowball. Someone had already placed a sandbox in the girls' room for the cat.

They made their plans to venture forth into the alley again and settled down to wait till all was quiet.

Chapter 5 / Out in the Night

Not long after Mandie and Celia went to their room, there was a knock on the door. Mandie opened it to find Miss Hope standing outside.

"Come in, Miss Hope," Mandie invited, opening the door wide.

Miss Hope remained in the hallway. "Thank you, Amanda, but I've only come to say that my sister asked if you would agree for Snowball to spend the night in the kitchen. She is hoping he will catch the mouse she thinks she heard in the wall. Mice automatically come to food, you know, and she thinks the kitchen would be the place it would go after everyone goes to bed and all the lights are out," she explained.

"Oh yes, of course, Miss Hope. I'll take him down to the kitchen," Mandie agreed.

"All the doors and windows are closed up and locked for the night, so I think he'll be safe, with no way to get outside," Miss Hope said.

"Oh, he probably wouldn't want to leave the warmth of the woodbox behind the stove," Mandie said with a little laugh. "But if a mouse does come within his smelling or hearing distance, he will go after it, I'm sure. I'll take him down right now." She turned toward the bed, where Snowball was curled up.

"That's all right, Amanda, I'll take him. I have to go back downstairs myself," Miss Hope told her.

"All right." Mandie went to pick him up and handed him over to Miss Hope. "If I were you I wouldn't set him down until you get to the kitchen. He might run off somewhere else, and then we'd have to search the house for him."

Miss Hope took the white cat in her arms. "I know very well he does just that," she said, "so I'll go straight to the kitchen. Aunt Phoebe has already gone to her house outside, but I alerted her that he might be in the kitchen when she comes in in the morning. Good night now, girls, both of you."

"Good night, Miss Hope," Mandie said, stroking her cat's head as Miss Hope held him.

"Good night," Celia called as Miss Hope started down the hallway.

Mandie closed the door. "I hope Snowball doesn't catch a rat tonight, or Miss Prudence might declare his work done and send him back to Grandmother's." She crossed the room to sit in one of the big chairs.

"Mandie, I've been thinking about your locket," Celia said, joining her in the other chair. "How can you be sure you lost it in the alley? Maybe it fell off in Mr. Heyward's store."

"No, I've figured it all out," Mandie replied. "When we turned around to run back to the store, when that man in the alley scared us, remember I ran into a tree limb and my collar got tangled up in it? I'm sure I lost it then."

"Oh goodness, Mandie, that man was watching us! He might have seen it happen and taken it himself," Celia said, her eyes wide.

"I hope not, Celia. That's why I need to go back and look for it as soon as possible, before someone does pick it up," Mandie answered.

"Do you think we can find the way to the alley from here?" Celia asked.

"Oh sure," Mandie replied. "Remember, King Street is a long street. It crosses this one, so if we walk toward downtown from here, we'll come to it, and then we'll just walk down King Street."

At that moment the old iron bell in the backyard of the schoolhouse rang out for curfew. Celia hurried to the string hanging down from the single lightbulb in the ceiling, gave it a yank, and turned off the light. Mandie blew out the oil lamp sitting on the table.

"Let's leave that lamp on by the bed," Mandie said. "If we close the curtains, it won't be seen in case someone is in the yard. And I think we ought to wait a few minutes just in case someone is still up," Mandie said, flopping back down in the chair.

"Let's don't wait too long, Mandie, or it will be awfully late by the time we get to bed tonight," Celia reminded her. She, too, sat down again.

"All right, let's wait thirty minutes and then we'll go," Mandie agreed, turning to squint at the clock on the mantelpiece in the dim lamplight.

"It's five minutes after ten," Celia told her. She was nearer to the clock.

"The bell rang at ten. So we'll leave at ten-thirty," Mandie decided.

At ten-thirty the girls slipped into their coats and hats, moving as quickly as they could. The cloaks they had worn earlier that day would be too bulky, they had decided. They could move faster in their coats.

They carefully made their way downstairs and to the backdoor in the hallway. For some reason the lamp that usually burned all night in the hallway was not lit. But Mandie knew the area well, and she quietly opened the door to a pantry by the back door. Cautiously stepping inside, she felt around until her hand came in contact with a lantern that she knew was kept there. Running her hand along the shelf above it, she found matches and quickly put them in her coat pocket.

Celia, waiting outside the door, wordlessly reached out to touch the lantern. Mandie bent near her and whispered in her ear, "I have the lantern and the matches. Let's go."

Celia went ahead and unlocked the back door, stepping aside for Mandie to go outside. She followed and pulled the door shut.

The two girls gingerly made their way through the tall shrubbery to the front of the house and then hurried down the front walkway to the road.

As soon as they were out of sight of the schoolhouse, Mandie blew out a long breath and said, "Now, if we can only get back in without disturbing anyone."

"Yes," Celia agreed, walking fast to keep up with her friend.

Just as they got to the corner of King Street, the two girls heard a loud meow behind them. Mandie looked back with a groan. "That can't be Snowball!" she said.

"But it is," Celia told her, peering through the darkness.

Snowball came bouncing up to his mistress in the dim moonlight and meowed loudly as he caught up with her.

"Snowball, how did you get out?" Mandie scolded. "You are supposed to be locked in the kitchen." The cat sat down and looked up at her, head cocked to one side.

"Somebody must have let him out," Celia said.

"I don't know. If someone let him out, then they might have seen us. I sure didn't see anyone when we left the schoolhouse, did you?" Mandie asked anxiously.

"No, not a soul," Celia replied. "What are we going to do now?"

Mandie shook her head doubtfully. "We're about halfway there, so I suppose we'll just go on and Snowball can come with us." She looked down at the cat and said, "Come on, Snowball, let's go. And mind me, you'd better not run off because I don't have time to chase you." She straightened up and continued down the street, swinging the unlit lantern.

Snowball seemed to understand that his mistress was disgusted with him. He stayed close to her feet as they walked, and once in a while he made a soft meowing sound.

When the girls came within sight of the alley, they paused to peer into it. The alley looked awfully dark. The tall old buildings were close together, and the roadway was very narrow, shutting out almost all the moonlight.

"Let's stay real close together, Mandie," Celia said in a whisper even though there was no indication anyone was around to hear at that time of night.

"All right, as soon as we get partway into the alley, I will light the lantern so we can look for the locket. I'll put it out when we start back so if anyone *is* around, they won't be able to see us for very long," Mandie said, starting forward.

"All right," Celia agreed, hovering close by.

Snowball began sniffing as they entered the alley, and Mandie immediately picked him up. "You are not going to run off, Snowball. There are lots of nasty things to smell in this old alley," she said, holding on to the lantern in the other hand.

"Mandie, let me hold him," Celia offered, reaching out to take the white cat. "You have to light the lantern and carry it."

As Mandie handed Snowball over, she said, "Please keep a good grip on him. If he picks up any interesting smells, he'll do all he can to get down."

"I will," Celia promised, holding Snowball with both arms.

Mandie stooped and lit the lantern with a match from her pocket. Flashing the light around, she bent over and began looking at the ground near the tree that had caught her collar earlier that day. She inspected the limbs and moved around in circles where the locket could have possibly fallen.

Celia squeezed Snowball tightly in her arms, causing him to wiggle in an attempt to get down as she bent over to help search.

"I'm afraid we are not going to find it," Mandie finally said with a sad sigh.

"It could have been thrown farther if that tree limb snapped it and flew back," Celia remarked as she moved away, bending over to look again.

Suddenly, Snowball found the right moment to escape Celia's arms. But he didn't run away. He sat near Mandie's feet and began washing his face and paws.

"Oh, Snowball, you'd better not run off." Mandie shook her head at him.

"Should I pick him up again?" Celia asked.

"I think he'll be all right," Mandie replied. "Just help me watch him in case he does decide to wander off."

"All right, Mandie. I can watch him for you while you hold the lantern," Celia promised. She kept searching for the locket, but she also kept Snowball within view.

The girls searched nearly every inch of the alley near the tree that had caught Mandie's collar. There was lots of old trash of every kind but no sign of the gold locket.

Mandie finally straightened up and looked around. "I'm so sure I lost it here. Someone else must have found it," she said, tears filling her blue eyes. "That was the only picture I had of my father, the one inside the locket. Celia, I don't know where else to look."

"Mandie, if you *didn't* lose it when the tree limb

hit you, it could have fallen off as we left here. And of course that would mean searching the whole road we walked on this afternoon," Celia told her.

"You're right," Mandie sighed. She looked up and down the alley. "We only came to right about here. We didn't go all the way down the alley, remember? So if we start here and work our way back toward Mr. Heyward's store, we would be following the path we took this afternoon."

At that moment Mandie saw Snowball bristle up his fur and freeze in his tracks. Almost immediately there came the sound of a dog barking in the distance.

"Quick, Celia, take the lantern," Mandie said, holding it out to her. She bent at the same time and scooped up Snowball. "Let's go."

The lantern swinging in Celia's hand, the girls almost ran up the alley in the direction they had come. The barking grew more distant.

Finally reaching the corner at King Street, they slowed down to catch their breath.

"I do believe that dog would have come after Snowball," Mandie gasped, "and we would have been in a real mess alone in that dark alley." She clutched Snowball on her shoulder.

"It sounded to me like the dog might have been shut in one of those buildings and couldn't get out." Celia commented between breaths as she straightened her skirt with her free hand.

"Anyhow, I think we were finished looking there," Mandie said, still firmly grasping the white cat. "We are almost to the back door of Mr. Heyward's store, so we could go on and look that far.

Then I suppose we'll have to go back to the school."

Celia still carried the lantern, and she kept moving it to shine on the ground as they searched. They finally arrived at the back door of the store.

"Might as well put out the light, and we'll go on back to our room," Mandie told her in a dejected tone.

Celia quickly extinguished the lantern, and they hurried up the street on their way back.

Just as they reached the driveway entrance to the school, Mandie put out a hand to stop Celia. "Since Miss Hope left Snowball in the kitchen, you open the door when we get inside the house and I'll shove him in," she instructed.

"All right," Celia agreed. "And we'd better be awfully quiet."

When they got around to the backyard, Celia pushed open the back door to the schoolhouse. Both girls quietly slipped inside, and Celia closed the door behind them and turned the key in the lock. Crossing the hall, Celia opened the kitchen door. Mandie gave Snowball a big push into the room and quickly closed the door.

Mandie silently took the lantern from Celia and returned it to the pantry where she had found it. Then the girls softly made their way up the stairs to their room on the third floor. There wasn't a sound in the house.

Finally reaching their room without being seen, the girls quickly began undressing for bed.

"I'm sorry you didn't find the locket, Mandie," Celia told her as she removed her long skirt and hung it up in the wardrobe.

"I suppose I'll never find it now," Mandie said sadly. She also hung up the dress she had been wearing. She paused and sat on the arm of one of the chairs, holding her nightgown. "You know, Celia, I really shouldn't have been wearing that locket everywhere I go—all the time, every day, and all. I should have kept it locked up in my jewelry box." She slowly moved her long blond braid of hair from her shoulder.

Celia sat on the opposite arm while she started to pull on her long, embroidered nightgown. "We do lots of things that we shouldn't do and don't realize it, Mandie, until something like this happens. It seems impossible to remember everything that we should do or shouldn't do."

Mandie shivered suddenly. "I think it's cold in here, don't you? Uncle Cal must not have sent up much heat in that radiator over there tonight. I think I'll just leave on my camisole and put my nightgown over it. It'll be warmer that way." She shook out the folds of the long nightgown.

"Me too, Mandie," Celia agreed, quickly sliding off the chair to straighten out her own nightgown. She became tangled in the folds and tripped, causing her to bump into Mandie. "Oh, I'm sorry," she apologized.

"That's all right," Mandie replied, standing up to finish dressing for bed.

Suddenly Celia was bumping into Mandie again, excitedly saying, "Wait, Mandie, wait!" She was pulling at Mandie's nightgown.

"Celia, what's wrong?" Mandie quickly demanded, stepping away from Celia's grasp.

"Mandie, look!" Celia was still excited as she

pointed to Mandie's camisole. "Look, there's the chain to your locket. Look there!"

Mandie quickly felt around her neck and the camisole. Her fingers touched the cold chain. She pulled it out from between the garments, looked at it, and then began searching again. "The locket! Here it is!" she cried, pulling it from the folds of the cloth.

"Oh, Mandie, I'm so glad!" Celia said, reaching forward to embrace her friend.

"Thanks, Celia," Mandie said, tightly clasping the locket and the chain as she returned the hug. Then she straightened up to examine the jewelry. "The chain is broken, look." She held it up to show the clasp was missing.

"So that tree limb did break the chain when you ran into it," Celia noted.

"Oh, thank the Lord," Mandie cried, squeezing the locket and broken chain in her hand. Then looking down at it, she immediately added, "And this gets locked up right now." She went to her jewelry box on the dresser. Taking the key out of her scarves in the bureau drawer where she kept it hidden, she unlocked the box and put the locket and chain inside.

"That is a very wise thing to do, Mandie," Celia said, watching her.

After Mandie had locked the jewelry box back up and returned the key to its hiding place, she quickly put on her nightgown. The two girls raced for the bed and jumped in under the covers.

Raising up on her elbow, Mandie said, "Think of all the trouble we went to—and the locket was in my clothes all the time. If I had just changed dresses before we went out, I would have found it."

"Yes, and now I suppose we are finished with that alley," Celia replied hopefully.

"Oh no," Mandie said. "We haven't found that puppy we heard crying the first time we went through there. The barking we heard tonight was from a bigger dog. I'd still like to find the puppy."

"Oh, Mandie, let's don't even talk about it right now," Celia moaned.

"There are other things, too, that we need to look into," Mandie reminded her. "How did Snowball get out of the kitchen? And as far as that alley is concerned, I'd still like to find out what's in all those old buildings down there."

"Mandie, you not only look for mysteries, you look for trouble," Celia replied with a laugh.

"Not really—it just seems like mysteries come to me sometimes," Mandie said, laughing as she lay down.

Tomorrow she would start planning her next investigation.

Chapter 6 / Unexpected Visitor

Mandie and Celia were busy almost all the next day with lessons and homework. When they were finished about three-thirty, they went for a stroll in the front yard. Though the sun was shining, the wind made it chilly enough for coats. Some of the other students at the school were also out for a breath of fresh air.

"Let's walk down near the road where we can talk," Mandie told Celia, glancing around at the other young ladies close to the front porch.

"Yes, let's do," Celia agreed.

Gradually moving down the hill, Mandie and Celia came to the bench under a huge magnolia tree near the end of the driveway. They sat down.

"I still want to go back to the alley, Celia, to see if I can find the puppy we heard whining the first time we went through there," Mandie said. "I'm trying to figure out when and how we can do it."

"Mandie, don't forget, we don't know yet whether Miss Prudence told your grandmother about us and that alley," Celia reminded her. "And if she did and if we go back in it again, that will mean we'll be in even more trouble."

"I don't believe she did," Mandie said. "Otherwise Grandmother would have said something." She frowned and added, "But if she didn't tell, I can't imagine why she didn't because she was really upset with us."

"Maybe she didn't get the right opportunity to talk to your grandmother because Aunt Rebecca was there," Celia suggested. "And now when Aunt Rebecca has gone home, Miss Prudence is ill with a cold or something. Just wait until she is up and out again. Then we'll know."

"I'm positive Grandmother will say something to me if and when Miss Prudence tells her anything. Grandmother won't just let it go," Mandie said.

"But we haven't seen your grandmother since we went to her dinner that night," Celia argued.

"I know, but believe me, if Grandmother hears about anything I've said or done, she will make a point to send for me," Mandie replied. "I still don't believe Miss Prudence told her anything about the alley."

"Knowing Miss Prudence, I would say that, sooner or later, she will be sure your grandmother knows about it," Celia said with a sigh.

"I have an idea," Mandie said, quickly turning to look at her friend. "We could go visit Grandmother, without waiting for her to send for us, while Miss Prudence is ill. Let's go find Miss Hope and get permission to go tomorrow. We don't have many classes tomorrow, so we can leave early enough to go and get back before dark." She stood up.

Celia rose, too. "All right, Mandie, but exactly what are you planning on doing? Going to your grandmother's and telling her about the alley before Miss Prudence can talk to her?"

Mandie started up the hill toward the front porch. "I don't know, Celia. I'll just see how I feel when I get there and how Grandmother acts."

They found Miss Hope in her office with what looked like a lot of work on her desk. She looked up and smiled when the girls stopped in the open doorway.

"Come in, Amanda, Celia," Miss Hope invited.

"Miss Hope," Mandie began as she and Celia entered the office. Then she stopped in surprise. "Snowball, what are you doing in here?" she said to the cat, who was sitting on a chair near the desk.

"I brought him in here so I could keep track of him," Miss Hope explained. "My sister is still hearing sounds like a mouse gnawing on something in the walls between her room and the hallway. So I thought perhaps Snowball might root it out for us. Now, what did you girls want?"

Snowball sat quietly in the chair, staring at his mistress.

"Miss Hope, I wanted to ask permission to go visit my grandmother tomorrow afternoon after classes are over—probably stay for supper at her house," Mandie answered, still watching her white cat.

"Of course, dear," Miss Hope agreed. Looking at Celia, she asked, "I suppose you want to go with her, do you, Celia?"

"Oh yes, ma'am, please," Celia answered with a smile.

"Fine then," Miss Hope said. "I'll ask Uncle Cal to drive you young ladies over there, and your grandmother's driver can bring you back. Now, you must let Uncle Cal know for sure whether you are staying for supper at Mrs. Taft's so I will know where you are."

"Yes, ma'am, thank you," Mandie said with a big smile. "As soon as we get to Grandmother's, I'll ask her if we should stay for supper and will tell Uncle Cal. Thank you, Miss Hope."

"Yes, thank you, Miss Hope," Celia said. "How is Miss Prudence today?"

"Still not well, I'm afraid, but she should be up and around in a few days," Miss Hope told her. "However, she is keeping up with everything that's going on here in the school while she's confined to her room. So, girls, please don't do anything you shouldn't while you are away from school tomorrow."

"Yes, ma'am, we won't," Mandie replied.

"We'll behave, Miss Hope," Celia said.

The girls went up to their room to freshen up for supper.

"Mandie, I have a feeling you are planning something that I don't know about," Celia said as she quickly brushed her auburn curls.

"No, Celia, but if we are late coming back, I can ask Ben to take the shortcut so we won't be late for curfew," Mandie said with a grin.

Celia looked at her. "Mandie, is that what you've been planning all along with this visit to your grandmother's? Because if it is, I'm not sure I want to go." She tightened her lips and frowned.

"No, no, Celia," Mandie quickly assured her. She closed the wardrobe door and turned to look at Celia. "That is not the reason I want to go to my grandmother's. I just want to see how she seems, whether I can figure out if Miss Prudence told her anything. And I promise we won't take the shortcut back unless you agree to it. I want you to go with me. Please?"

"Well, all right—that is, if you keep your promise not to ask Ben to drive us back through that alley," Celia said slowly.

"All right, all right, I promise," Mandie said with a big sigh. "Now, let's go downstairs. It's almost time for supper."

After supper the girls went back to their room and read for a while.

Mandie caught herself nodding as her book slipped out of her hands. She straightened up, yawned, and said, "I think I'll go to bed."

"Me too," Celia agreed, closing her book and glancing at the clock on the mantel. "It's twenty minutes to ten anyway."

"Yes, let's hit the hay," Mandie said with a laugh. She put out the oil lamp nearby as Celia pulled the string to turn off the light bulb dangling from the ceiling.

They jumped into the big bed, and both girls were soon fast asleep.

In Mandie's dream someone was knocking on their door. Then she suddenly came awake and sat up. She wasn't dreaming. Someone was tapping on their window. How could that be? They were on the third floor.

Celia asked sleepily, "What is that noise, Mandie?" She rubbed her eyes and raised up to look around.

"There's someone outside our window," Mandie whispered. She pushed back the covers and got out of bed. She cautiously crept across the dark room toward the window.

"How could someone be outside our window, Mandie? We're on the third floor," Celia whispered back, right behind her.

"Exactly what I was thinking," Mandie said softly. She approached the window from the side, hoping whoever was out there could not see her until she discovered who it was. Celia peered over Mandie's shoulder.

Suddenly there was a much louder tapping at the window, and Mandie was afraid the window glass was going to break. This made her angry, and she called out, "Who is that? Who's out there?"

The tapping continued, but no one answered. Mandie slowly leaned forward enough to see outside. The moon was shining, but clouds were drifting over it. Their window was set into the sloping roof with a two-foot ledge outside the sill. She caught a glimpse of someone on the limb of the huge magnolia tree outside their window. Whoever it was leaned forward now and then to tap their window with a long branch.

"Someone hanging on a limb of the tree," Mandie whispered to Celia.

When the tapping began again, Mandie quickly raised the window and called out, "Go away, whoever you are, or I'll get someone to make you get out of that tree. You hear?"

The answer came quickly with a laugh. "Ah, now you be awake. Now, you just wait. I'm coming inside. Don't you be closing that window," a voice said.

"Mollie! What are you doing in that tree?" Mandie asked as she recognized the voice. She leaned out. Sure enough, it was Mollie. And Mollie was hastily crawling along the big limb toward the window. "Mollie, don't do that. You'll fall!"

"If I be falling, Hilda will catch me below. She promised," Mollie called back as she continued moving along the limb.

"Hilda too!" Celia exclaimed over Mandie's shoulder.

The two girls looked down but couldn't see directly beneath the window. "I'll come down there, Mollie," Mandie told her. "You go back down the tree to Hilda and wait for me."

"No, Mandie, I be coming to your room, that I am," Mollie argued.

"Oh no, what are we going to do? That limb doesn't reach all the way to the window. She'll fall!" Mandie said to Celia.

"We could call someone to help," Celia suggested.

"Not enough time," Mandie replied, watching every move Mollie made.

Mollie reached the end of the limb and immediately climbed onto the next one above, which was longer and closer to the window. It was also stronger, and she managed to get to the end of it.

"Catch me, Mandie! I be jumping in your window!" Mollie called out.

"No, no, no! Mollie, you can't do that! Stop!" Mandie called to her.

Mollie ignored the warning and made a jump at the window. She missed but managed to grab hold of the previous branch. She was dangling in the air and couldn't seem to get back onto the limb.

"The bed sheet!" Mandie cried out. She rushed to pull the sheet off the bed.

Celia quickly helped her tie a big knot in one corner of the sheet. They rushed back to the window and swung the sheet over the windowsill.

"Mollie, when we swing this out, you grab it and hold on for everything you're worth. Don't dare let go of it! You hear me?" Mandie called to the girl.

"I be hearing," Mollie replied. "Just you be hurrying, Mandie."

Together Mandie and Celia tossed the knotted end of the sheet as far as they could. It missed the small figure by inches. They tried again, and this time Mollie managed to grab hold with one hand.

"Hold tight, Mollie! We're going to pull you inside," Mandie called to her as she leaned farther out the window. Mollie was dangling below them at the end of the sheet. Mandie grasped it tightly and crawled out onto the ledge. Looking back at Celia, she said, "Now, all together!"

The two girls pulled with all their might, and Mollie's head appeared at the edge of the ledge. Mandie caught one of her hands and slowly helped the little girl up over the ledge. The three of them fell on the floor of the bedroom.

Mollie jumped up and laughingly said, "That was fun, now, sure enough it was!"

Mandie and Celia, both completely out of

breath after the dangerous rescue, sat on the floor staring at Mollie.

Mandie took a deep breath and said, "Mollie, if you ever try anything like that again, I will see that you end up in deep trouble. I'll ask Grandmother to lock you in your room at night so you can't get out. Do you understand?" Mandie was angry and had all she could do to control her voice.

Mollie frowned and sat on the floor next to the girls. "Oh, Mandie, I only be wanting to come see you. And Hilda showed me which window. She said she used to live in this schoolhouse," the little orphan explained.

"Hilda can't talk. You know that, Mollie, so you must be just making all this up," Mandie replied.

"But I told Hilda I wanted to come see you, and she came with me to show me the way. And then when we be down under the tree below she pointed to this window," Mollie explained.

Mandie and Celia looked at each other, realizing that Hilda indeed would know which room was theirs. The waif had been living in the school attic when they found her after they had first arrived at the school a long time ago.

"Hilda!" Mandie suddenly remembered. "She's still down in the yard. I hope she doesn't try to climb that tree." She stood to her feet and looked at Celia. "I suppose I'm going to have to get dressed and take them back to Grandmother's."

"Mandie, why don't we wake Uncle Cal or someone and get them to go with us. It's awfully late, and we aren't supposed to be out," Celia said doubtfully.

"I'm not afraid," Mandie told her as she hastily

took down a dress from the wardrobe.

Celia came to join her. "If you're going, then I'll go with you," she said. She grabbed a dress and began putting it on.

Mollie watched the two, looking from one to the other during their conversation. "Now, Mandie, Hilda be knowing the way back, she does," she said. "Just find me the way out of this house. I go back with Hilda."

"Oh no, you don't!" Mandie said sharply as she put on her shoes. "We are going back with you to be sure you get back safely. And please remember what I said. If you ever do such a thing again, I'll speak to Grandmother."

"Yes, Mandie, you already be telling me that," Mollie replied.

"Ready?" Mandie asked Celia, her hand on the doorknob.

"Yes," Celia replied, pulling on her coat.

"Now, Mollie, we are going down the back stairway and out the back door. Don't you dare make a sound," Mandie told the girl. "If anyone sees or hears us, you're going to be in much deeper trouble, understand?"

"I understand what trouble be, that I do," Mollie replied, moving to stand close behind her.

"Not a word, not a sound," Mandie warned, then softly opened the door. The three of them stepped out into the hall.

They got down the back stairs without incident. Mandie led the way around the house to the yard beneath their window to look for Hilda. She found the girl curled up, asleep on the bench beneath the magnolia tree.

"Hilda, let's go home," Mandie said, softly touching her head.

Hilda instantly jumped up and ran down the driveway. Mollie started to run after her, but Mandie grabbed her hand and held it tight.

"You are not running away. We are going to Grandmother's house," Mandie told her.

"But Hilda be gone," Mollie said, pointing.

"No, she's not," Mandie said. She nodded toward the girl, who was waiting for them down at the road.

"But she will be gone again," Mollie replied.

And, sure enough, as soon as the three caught up with Hilda, the girl once more ran ahead. Mandie noticed she did seem to know the way and that she would go ahead and then look back to see if they were following.

Finally they arrived at Mrs. Taft's house. The moon was still playing hide-and-seek behind the clouds. Mandie tried to determine if anyone was up and about in the house, but she couldn't see a light inside. They paused in the front driveway. Hilda waited just ahead of them.

"What do we do now?" Celia asked in a whisper.

"We be going inside," Mollie declared and tried to pull away from Mandie.

Mandie held her hand firmly and said, "We have to figure out how to get you back in the house without waking anyone, or you will most certainly be in trouble."

"Why don't we go around to the back and see if there are any lights on in the back of the house?" Celia suggested.

"Yes, let's do," Mandie agreed. Looking at Hilda, she said, "Come on with us, Hilda. We are going in the house."

Hilda immediately ran down the driveway toward the back of the house. Mollie tried to pull away again. "I be going with Hilda," she repeated.

"No!" Mandie said, holding on to her hand ever more tightly.

Mandie and Celia walked on with Mollie around the house. When they came to the back door Mandie was shocked to see her grandmother standing in the doorway talking to Ben. "Grandmother!" she exclaimed at the same instant Mrs. Taft saw them.

"Well, now, I see y'all have found her," Mrs. Taft said. Then with sudden alarm, she said, "She didn't come to the school in the middle of the night, did she?"

"Yes, Grandmother, she did. And Hilda was with her. She ran ahead of us, but she's around here somewhere, too," Mandie explained, finally letting go of Mollie's hand.

Mollie immediately tried to go in the back door, but Mrs. Taft grabbed the back of her dress to stop her. "Not so fast now, Mollie," she scolded. "You have done something bad, and you will be punished for it. You just wait here, because I am going to see that you are confined to your room for the rest of the night." She looked out into the yard and added, "And, Hilda, you come on here. We are going back to bed."

Hilda immediately came out of the shadows, darted past Mrs. Taft, and disappeared into the house.

"Now, girls, Ben will take you back to school,"

Mrs. Taft said. "I was just going to send him out looking for these two." She turned to her driver. "Ben, see that the girls get back safely."

"Yessum, Miz Taft, dat I do," Ben replied. "Already got de buggy hitched up in de barn." He went to get it.

"Grandmother, you wouldn't believe what Mollie did," Mandie began.

"It's late now, dear. You girls get on back to school before you are missed, and we can talk later," Mrs. Taft said as Ben drove the buggy up.

"We've already got permission to come to see you tomorrow afternoon, so we can talk then," Mandie told her. "Good night, Grandmother."

Mrs. Taft started to go inside and close the door. She stepped back and called to Mandie as she and Celia climbed into the buggy. "Just let me know if there's any trouble at school regarding this escapade. Good night, now."

"Yes, Grandmother, we will," Mandie promised.

Ben drove fast and they were soon nearing the school.

"Stop here on the road," Mandie instructed. "Someone might hear the buggy if you go up the driveway."

Ben stopped the horse and the girls jumped out. "I'll be waitin' right heah till you all gits in de house, now," he told them.

"Thank you, Ben," Mandie replied. "We're going in the back, so you won't be able to see us."

She and Celia rushed up the driveway and waved as they ran around the house to the back door.

Once in their room, the girls almost collapsed

before they could get undressed and back into bed again. They had to recover their sheet and put it back on and then crawled in. It had been an adventure they would not want to repeat.

Chapter 7 / Bad News

The excitement of the night before left the girls tired and groggy the next morning. But eventually time came to visit Mrs. Taft. When Ben came to pick them up, the girls were waiting in the foyer. He had brought a note to Miss Hope from Mrs. Taft.

"Miz Taft, she say fo' you to give dis heah note to Miss Hope," Ben told Mandie, holding out a small white envelope.

Mandie took it. "I wonder what's in this," she said as she stared at the envelope in her hand.

"I knows whut dat be," Ben explained, nodding his head. "Miz Taft, she tell Miss Hope you young ladies gwine stay at her house till Sunday night since today be Friday."

Mandie immediately realized this would put her plans for visiting the alley on hold. She would have to wait until next week for another chance.

"What do you say, Celia? Want to stay till Sunday night?" she asked her friend.

Celia smiled. "Of course, Mandie. I always enjoy visiting at your grandmother's house. And besides, Mollie is still there."

Mandie rolled her eyes and groaned. "Yes, and she will probably keep the weekend in a turmoil." Turning back to Ben, she said, "I'll have to give this to Miss Hope, and if she says we may stay, then we'll have to run back to our room and get some clothes to take with us. All right?"

"I waits," Ben agreed, smiling at her. "I seen Uncle Cal in de yard. I goes and talks to him whilst I waits." He turned to go back out the door.

"Thanks. We'll hurry," Mandie promised.

Miss Hope gave permission, and the girls quickly put their things in a bag. As they finished, someone knocked on their door. Mandie opened it.

Aunt Phoebe was holding Snowball in her arms. "Miss Hope, she say you take dis heah cat wid y'all so she won't hafta tend to him whilst y'all gone," she announced.

Mandie reached for the cat. "Then she must have decided she doesn't need him here anymore," she said.

"Oh no, missy, she say fo' you to bring him back when you comes back," Aunt Phoebe explained.

Mandie smiled. "Please tell Miss Hope I will," she assured the woman.

When they finally arrived at Mrs. Taft's house, Mollie was overjoyed to see the white cat. She had come to the front door with Ella, the maid, who let them in.

"Mandie, I be glad you be bringing Snowball,"

Mollie said, smiling joyfully as Mandie put Snowball down in the front hallway.

Snowball took one look at Mollie and quickly disappeared down the corridor. Mollie ran after him.

"I'm not so sure Snowball is glad to see Mollie," Mandie laughed as she removed her coat.

"Dat white cat, he run like dat everytime he see dat little girl." Ella laughed, too. "But he jes' be playin' wid huh, 'cause he keep lookin' back to see if she comin' after him."

"Miss Hope wanted me to bring him with me and then take him back when we go," Mandie explained. "He hasn't found that rat that Miss Prudence says she keeps hearing."

"I take yo' bag to yo' room," Ella said, reaching for it. Ben had set it inside the door for them. "Miz Taft, she in de parlor now."

"Thank you, Ella," Mandie said as she and Celia hung their coats and hats on the hall tree.

Mrs. Taft was sitting by the fireplace. Mandie and Celia pulled up low stools near the crackling fire.

"Grandmother, why do you still build a fire in the fireplace now that you've got the new furnace?"

"Oh, my dear," Mrs. Taft replied. "Those furnaces are good for heat, but they make the most awful racket sometimes, hissing and clanking. So unless it is terribly cold outside, I tell Ben to leave it alone and build a fire here instead." Her tone turned brisk. "Now, while the child is nowhere in sight, tell me what you were talking about last night."

"Oh, Grandmother, Mollie did the most dangerous thing," Mandie began, and she related the happenings of the night before.

"Oh dear, I suppose I'll have to ask Ella to keep her within her sight every minute she is here. I didn't realize she would try such dangerous things," Mrs. Taft said, shaking her head. "I thought it would be nice for Hilda to have her come and visit, but now I just don't know. She may influence Hilda to do some of those dangerous escapades."

"When is Aunt Rebecca coming back after her?" Celia asked.

"Next weekend, unless I let her know otherwise," Mrs. Taft replied. "And you know Mollie is studying part of every day with Mrs. Manning's daughter, who has a private tutor, so I won't be able to keep track of her every minute."

"Maybe Ella could go and stay with her when she goes to Mrs. Manning's," Mandie suggested.

"Yes, I suppose Ella could," Mrs. Taft replied. "I'm worried about her getting into something that is dangerous and getting hurt—or worse." Looking at Celia, she asked, "Does your aunt Rebecca not have any trouble of this kind with her?"

"Not that I know of," Celia replied.

At that moment Ella came to the doorway of the parlor. "Supper is on de table, Miz Taft," she announced. "Annie done got Hilda and Mollie in de sitting room to eat their supper." Annie was Mrs. Taft's other maid.

"Thank you, Ella," Mrs. Taft said, rising from her chair. "Let's go eat, girls." As she left the room, she looked back and said, "And we can talk without Mollie taking over the conversation." She smiled.

Mandie and Celia followed Mrs. Taft into the dining room. As everyone sat down, Mrs. Taft glanced at the buffet and said to Ella, "I see Mrs. Manning has come to pick up the silver set."

Ella frowned and said, "I ain't seen Mrs. Manning this week. She musta come and got it while I was not around."

"You haven't seen Mrs. Manning this week?" Mrs. Taft repeated. "But I haven't seen her, either. Ben has been taking Mollie and Hilda over there for lessons every day." She walked over to the buffet and looked around. "She wouldn't have simply walked in and taken the set without saying anything. I wonder what happened to it, then."

"I don't be knowing, Miz Taft," Ella said, staring at the buffet. "I sho' didn't move it. It was right there until yesterday mornin' when I came back from de store. Then I noticed it was gone."

"Yesterday? I was here all day except for that tea Mrs. Simms had at noon yesterday," Mrs. Taft said thoughtfully.

Mandie spoke up, "Maybe Mrs. Manning came while both you and Ella were gone, Grandmother, and Annie let her have it."

Mrs. Taft shook her head. "No, I gave Annie the day off yesterday to go visit her sister. She left early in the morning and didn't return until after dark last night."

Celia cleared her throat and asked slowly, "You don't think Mollie could have moved it, do you?"

"No, Ben took Mollie and Hilda over to the Mannings' early yesterday because I was going

out, and they didn't get back until after I returned,"
Mrs. Taft replied. She went back to the table and
sat down looking perplexed.

"What day was Mrs. Manning going to have
that dinner at her church, when she would be need-
ing to borrow the set?" Mandie asked.

"That dinner is scheduled for tomorrow night,"
Mrs. Taft told her. "Well, let's eat while the food is
hot." She started passing the bowls around the
table while Ella poured the coffee.

As they ate, Mandie was busy trying to figure
out what had happened to the silver set. She also
kept waiting for Mrs. Taft to say something about
their ride through the forbidden alley last Sunday
night. By the time the meal was over, she had decided her grandmother did not know anything
about it. Miss Prudence must not have mentioned
the incident during her visit with Mrs. Taft.

Later that night when everyone had retired,
Mandie and Celia lay awake in the room they
shared discussing the disappearance of the silver
tea set.

"Someone had to take it. It couldn't just leave
by itself," Mandie declared, pushing up on her pillow.

"Yes, definitely someone had to take it. But
who, Mandie?" Celia wondered.

"Everyone was gone. Grandmother was at that
tea, Ella had gone on an errand at that time, and
Annie had the day off," Mandie said, listing off the
people in the household.

"What about Ben? Where was he?" Celia
asked.

"He had driven Grandmother to the tea and

92

waited there," Mandie said.

"Well, there's Gabriel, who works in the yard," Celia remembered.

"No, he never comes in the house," Mandie told her.

"Do you think some stranger might have come in and taken it, then?" Celia asked.

"That's exactly what I was thinking," Mandie said. "However, I know Grandmother is very careful about locking up the house when she goes off. Someone would have had to break into the house, and Grandmother didn't say anything about that."

"Maybe they broke in somewhere that no one has noticed," Celia suggested.

"Maybe," Mandie agreed. "Tomorrow we should go through the whole house checking all the windows and doors to see if any of them have been forced open."

"I wish we had thought about doing that before we went to bed," Celia said. "This is such a big house and some of the rooms aren't used very often."

"If someone did break in, I suppose that silver set was all they wanted," Mandie said. "Grandmother didn't notice anything else missing. And from what Ella said, it must have happened yesterday, so whoever it was has been long gone."

Celia sat up in bed and looked around the dim light from the moon at the window. "Mandie, would you mind if I got up and locked our door?"

"I don't mind, Celia," Mandie told her. "Go ahead if it will make you feel any safer." She propped herself up against her pillow and watched Celia swing her legs off the bed.

"I'm going to check the window locks, too," Celia said, standing up.

"I'll help," Mandie told her as she slid out of bed.

While Celia locked the door to the hallway, Mandie pushed back the draperies and felt for the window locks. Every one was securely locked.

"Now everything is locked up tight," Mandie said, jumping back into bed.

"Yes, and this might serve another purpose, too," Celia said, getting back under the covers. "It will keep Mollie from barging in on us in the middle of the night."

"I think Grandmother has Annie staying in the room with Mollie and Hilda now so they can't run off somewhere," Mandie reminded her.

"Yes, but Annie has to sleep sometime, and Mollie is smart enough to take advantage of that," Celia said.

Suddenly, the radiator across the room began hissing and rattling, startling both girls until they realized what it was.

"That noisy old radiator, acting up at this time of the night!" Mandie exclaimed, taking a deep breath to slow her pounding heart.

"It sure picked a scary time to do it," Celia said, swallowing hard.

"Yes, and pretty soon it'll get so hot in here we'll have to start turning down the quilts," Mandie added. "Anyhow, I think we'd better go to sleep. Grandmother always expects us to be on time for breakfast, and she never sleeps late."

The girls finally went to sleep and didn't waken

again until morning, when someone softly tapped on their door.

Mandie raised up in bed and rubbed her eyes.

"Someone is knocking on the door," Celia said, climbing out of bed to investigate.

"It's probably Mollie," Mandie said.

But when Celia opened the door, it was Ella. "Miz Taft sent me to say breakfast in ten minutes," Ella told the girls.

"Ten minutes?" Mandie exclaimed, jumping out of bed. "We must have overslept." She rushed to the mantelpiece to look at the clock. "Oh, goodness, we did. It's ten minutes to eight. Thanks, Ella. Please tell Grandmother we'll be there on time." She ran for her clothes.

"She got more company, dis early in de mawnin'," Ella told the girls. "Dat big tall Injun man is here."

"Uncle Ned?" Mandie turned to quickly ask.

"He sho' is, so don't be late," Ella said as she closed the door behind her.

"Uncle Ned is here," Mandie repeated as she scrambled into her clothing. "I wonder if he came for a special reason, or just to visit."

"Maybe he is just traveling through and stopped to see you," Celia commented as she also hurried into her dress.

The girls rushed downstairs to the parlor, where Uncle Ned and Mrs. Taft sat talking. Snowball was curled up asleep on the hearth.

"Snowball!" Mandie exclaimed. "I completely forgot about you last night. You must have slept in the room with Mollie." Then looking at her father's old Cherokee friend, Uncle Ned, she said, "Good morning, Uncle Ned. You are out awfully early this morning." She sat down nearby.

Celia also pulled up a stool and bent to pet Snowball.

The old man smiled at her and said, "Come early to spread the word. Bad men stealing from people."

Mandie caught her breath. "Thieves?" she gasped.

"Yes, dear, from what Uncle Ned has told me, I believe that someone somehow managed to steal the silver set from the buffet," Mrs. Taft said.

"Lots of burglaries in this community," Uncle Ned explained.

"Where did you hear this, Uncle Ned? How do you know?" Mandie asked.

"People tell sheriff things go missing," Uncle Ned explained.

Celia listened to every word. "You see, Mandie," she said, "it was a good idea to lock our door last night."

Mrs. Taft looked at the girls and asked, "You locked your bedroom door last night?"

"Yes, ma'am," Mandie said. "But it was mostly to keep Mollie from wandering in in the middle of the night."

"That might have been a good idea. However, Annie is staying with Mollie and Hilda every minute to see that they don't get into something else," Mrs. Taft assured her.

"What have these people been stealing, Uncle Ned?" Mandie asked.

"Small things like silver set, jewelry, things that can be easily hidden," he explained.

"But what are they going to do with the stuff that they steal? They couldn't sell it around here because someone would find out where it came from," Mandie said.

"Do not know," Uncle Ned replied. "Steal and hide somewhere maybe for later to sell."

"Uncle Ned has already been by your school and talked with Miss Hope," Mrs. Taft explained. "The schoolhouse will keep all its windows and doors locked until these thieves are caught. When you girls return tomorrow night, the doors will be locked and you will probably have to go get Aunt Phoebe or Uncle Cal in their house in the backyard to let you in."

"This sounds dangerous," Celia murmured.

"Uncle Ned has some of his young men keeping watch over the town, trying to help the sheriff catch them," Mrs. Taft explained.

"Grandmother, if these people stole your silver set, how did they get in? Don't you always lock the door when you go off?" Mandie asked.

"We haven't figured that out yet, dear," Mrs. Taft replied. "I'm going to send for Ben and Gabriel in a little while and have them search the whole yard, barns and all, and Uncle Ned will check the house for us."

"Can I help, Uncle Ned?" Mandie eagerly asked.

Uncle Ned shook his head and said, "Not safe. Two braves out back wait to help me search everywhere."

"But can't I help? I could stay right with you, Uncle Ned," Mandie begged.

Ella came to the door to announce that breakfast was ready, and everyone moved on into the breakfast room.

"We'll eat first, Uncle Ned," Mrs. Taft told him as she led the way.

No one wasted any time over breakfast, and they were soon finished. Mrs. Taft insisted the girls stay with her in the parlor while Uncle Ned and his two men searched the house from the basement up to the attic. After a long while the old man came back to report.

"No one anywhere," he said. "No sign of anyone anywhere." He came to sit by the fire while he explained.

"No sign of anyone? Then I wonder how someone managed to get inside this house and steal that silver set, Uncle Ned," Mrs. Taft said.

"Must have come through door somewhere," he said. "Some door must have been unlocked."

"I never go off anywhere and leave doors unlocked, Uncle Ned," Mrs. Taft told him. Then she added thoughtfully, "If a door was left unlocked, then one of the maids must have gone out and left it unlocked. I'd better speak to Ella and Annie."

"Maybe thief have key," the old man suggested.

"I don't know of anyone who has a key to my house," Mrs. Taft said.

"Maybe someone stole a key sometime or other," Mandie suggested.

"This is a puzzle to me," Mrs. Taft decided. "But we need to figure out how it happened so it won't happen again."

"Is the silver set the only thing that is missing, Grandmother?" Mandie asked.

"Why, yes, it's the only thing I have actually missed," Mrs. Taft replied. "But I probably need to take an inventory of everything."

"I'll help," Mandie quickly volunteered again.

"All right. I have a list of all the valuables in this house and it's in the wall safe. We can use that to check everything out," Mrs. Taft told her. "Then I will need to talk to the sheriff."

Mandie was anxious to get started. This would probably take a long time to do, and she wanted to do her own investigation. She had her own ideas about solving this mystery.

Chapter 8 / Uncle Ned Investigates

Mandie and Celia followed Mrs. Taft around the house as she looked for a writing tablet they could use to record the inventory.

Having no luck with the library desk drawer, the last place left where there might be a tablet, Mrs. Taft straightened up. "I never can remember to buy tablets, so I must be completely out," she said. "Would you girls want to go down to Heyward's Store and get some for me? Ben can drive you."

"Heyward's Store?" Mandie repeated. That was the store with the back door opening into the street leading to the alley. "Yes, ma'am, Grandmother. Celia and I can go get the tablets."

"Then I'll have Ben harness up the buggy," Mrs. Taft said, starting toward the hallway. "And you know to just tell Mr. Heyward to put these on my account, don't you?"

"Oh yes, ma'am," Mandie replied. "We've

made purchases for Miss Hope before, so we know how to do it."

"Get your cloaks. It's a little cold out there this morning," Mrs. Taft said.

"Yes, ma'am," both girls answered.

Mandie and Celia hurried up to their room for their wraps and were downstairs at the back door by the time Ben got the buggy ready.

"Ben, no side trips, now," Mrs. Taft was instructing him as he stood waiting by the vehicle in the driveway. "Straight to Heyward's Store and back. And wait for the girls. No wandering off while they shop, understand?"

"Yessum, Miz Taft, I understands," Ben replied. "We ain't goin' down no extry streets no mo'. Be back before you can shake a stick at a chicken."

Mandie listened to the conversation and wondered again whether her grandmother was aware of their shortcut through the alley that night.

"And, Ben, whoever the thieves are that are stealing in this town, they may be connected to that alley, so stay completely away from it," Mrs. Taft continued.

Mandie caught her breath and quickly looked at Celia, who was also listening. Her grandmother must know about the rig breaking down that night in the alley. But why had she not mentioned it to the girls?

"Dat Injun man left with his two men, Miz Taft, and he say tell you he go searchin' for thieves, but he be back later," Ben said.

"Yes, he told me he would. He wants to help find the thieves because some of the white people are always so ready to blame things on the Cherokee people," Mrs. Taft said. Turning to the girls, she said, "Now, hurry back. We need to get this inventory done, and it will take quite a while to do."

"Yes, ma'am," both girls answered again.

The two jumped up into the buggy, and as soon as they were on the road, Mandie began asking questions.

"Ben, did you tell Grandmother about our going through that dark alley?" Mandie asked.

Ben looked at Mandie, who was sitting in the middle, cleared his throat, and replied, "Dat I did, missy. Figured best to tell dat lady befo' she find out from somebody else."

Mandie blew out a breath of relief. "Thank goodness you did, Ben. My grandmother was not upset about it after all, was she?"

"Yo' grandma, she want to be de boss. She don't want dat school lady tellin' her things she don't know, so I figured I tell her befo' dat Miz Prudy git to it," Ben explained.

"I'm glad you did, Ben," Celia said.

"So you had already told her before we came over that night and Miss Prudence was there, too," Mandie said.

"Dat I did," Ben said. "Like dat Injun man always say, better to tell than wait fo' somebody else to tell it."

"What did my grandmother say, Ben?" Mandie pressed further as Ben drove around a corner of the downtown business section.

"She say, 'You do right, Ben, tellin' me,' " the driver replied. "And she say I must promise not to go back down dat alley agin, so I promised, so now we cain't ever go down it agin." He looked at Mandie, nodding and smiling.

"You promised, Ben," Mandie said. "Grandmother hasn't mentioned it to us, but she knows you drive us everywhere we want to go and that you will abide by her wishes. Why didn't you tell us that you had told her?"

Ben focused his attention back on the road and said, "I figures you won't be likin' dat 'cause now I cain't ever drive you through dat alley agin."

Mandie thought quickly for a response. "That's fine, Ben," she said. "You keep your promise to my grandmother." She glanced at Celia by her side.

Celia raised her eyebrows as she met Mandie's glance. Mandie knew what Celia was thinking because they had discussed it. Mrs. Taft had probably given Ben strict orders as to where exactly he could drive the girls from now on. They would not be allowed to persuade Ben off on side trips like they had been doing.

"Here we be, young ladies," Ben announced as he pulled the buggy up to a hitching post in front of Heyward's Store. "Now, Miz Taft, she say fo' me to wait right heah fo' y'all."

Mandie and Celia stepped down from the vehicle. "Yes, Ben, you wait right here," Mandie said. "We won't be but a few minutes."

As soon as the two girls entered the store, they began a mumbled conversation under their breath.

"What a relief to know that Grandmother is not going to give us any strict orders about where we can and can't go," Mandie said. "She's instructed Ben about it. So if we make a suggestion now and then, Ben might agree to take us other places, pro-

vided those places are in respectable neighbor-
hoods."

"Yes," Celia whispered back. "I was surprised
that your grandmother did not talk to us about that
alley."

"But remember, it wasn't our fault. And it
wasn't really Ben's, either, because the rig broke
down. If that had not happened, we would have
driven straight through there without any problem," Mandie replied.

Mr. Heyward was back at the desk, thanking a
customer who was leaving. The girls paused in the
aisle to wait. They were shocked when the customer turned to come down the aisle to the front
door.

"April Snow!" Mandie exclaimed at the same
moment she saw them.

Grasping her purchase, April rushed past them
without a word and on out the front door. Mandie
and Celia turned to look after her.

"She must be alone, which is strictly forbidden," Mandie whispered to Celia. She hurried to
look out the front door and saw April rush down the
street.

Celia came up behind Mandie and said, "I wonder what she bought."

Mr. Heyward had seen the two girls, and he
came down the aisle to greet them. "And how are
you young ladies today? Back for another purchase for Miss Hope?" he said.

"Oh, hello, Mr. Heyward. No, sir, we came for
my grandmother today," Mandie said, quickly
turning to look at the man.

"And how is Mrs. Taft today?" Mr. Heyward asked.

Mandie mentally debated whether to mention the burglaries to this man and then decided it would be all right to discuss it.

"Mr. Heyward, you have probably heard about the burglaries that are happening here in Asheville," Mandie began. "Well, my grandmother has a silver set missing, and she can't figure out where it got to."

"Oh dear!" Mr. Heyward replied. "Yes, I have heard about the burglaries and have been taking extra precautions to safeguard my store."

"Grandmother wants to take an inventory of all her possessions, and she doesn't have any writing tablets. So that's what we are here for," Mandie explained.

"I know exactly what type your grandmother buys," Mr. Heyward said, going over to shelves stacked with merchandise. He pulled out a stack of tablets and turned to ask, "How many of these would Mrs. Taft like?"

"She said I might as well get a dozen. That way she won't run out any time soon," Mandie replied.

"I don't have that many right here in this shelf, but I do in the stockroom. I just sold a dozen to Miss Snow, who just left. I believe she is from your school. Anyhow, if you young ladies will wait for me, I'll be right back," Mr. Heyward said, disappearing through a doorway.

Mandie quickly looked at Celia and said, "Let's go look out the back door while we wait." She rushed to the windowed door at the rear and gazed out at the streets beyond.

Celia peered over Mandie's shoulder. "Mandie, you are not thinking of going out into that alley again, are you?" Celia asked in a hoarse whisper.

Mandie hummed under her breath and then said, "No, not right now. I just wanted to see if any of those bums Tommy and Robert told us about happened to be wandering around in the streets back here. But I don't see anyone."

"Neither do I," Celia said.

"I would still like to find that puppy we heard in the alley that night," Mandie told her.

"Mandie, that puppy is probably long gone by now, and we shouldn't roam around down there again," Celia said nervously. "Besides, it could be dangerous. Those people stealing from everyone may be hiding out in that alley."

Mandie looked at her friend. "You are right, Celia. I wonder if Uncle Ned has looked in that alley, or the sheriff, or somebody—whoever is hunting the burglars."

"I don't think Uncle Ned said," Celia replied.

"You know, Celia, I just had an idea," Mandie said slowly. "That dark alley would be the perfect place for those burglars to hide their loot."

"Mandie!" Celia exclaimed. "We are not going in there to look for it."

"It would be awfully nice if we could recover Grandmother's silver set, because I'm sure it's very old and worth lots of money," Mandie said.

"We will let the lawmen recover it, Mandie," Celia insisted. "We are not going to get involved in dangerous things like that. I refuse."

"We've been in there before and nothing happened to us," Mandie argued.

"Oh no, not much! Remember that bum who spit at us and we had to run?" Celia reminded her.

"We wouldn't have to speak to him if we saw him again. Remember, he didn't bother us until we tried to talk to him," Mandie said.

"There may be dozens of men like him in that terrible place," Celia said.

"Maybe I could persuade Tommy Patton to go with me to investigate that place," Mandie said.

Mr. Heyward called to them down the aisle. "I have the order ready, young ladies. I'll take it out to Ben for you."

"Oh, thank you, Mr. Heyward," Mandie replied. Then, as the three of them walked toward the front door, Mandie asked, "Do bums really live in that old dark alley back there?"

Mr. Heyward looked at her and said, "It's definitely no place for young ladies like you two. That whole section back there needs to be torn down. It's a festering sore and a place for bums. Although that alley is a few blocks away, I even keep my back door locked now since hearing of the burglaries. I'm afraid some of those decrepit people may come into my store."

"I hope they find all the thieves," Mandie said.

Mr. Heyward opened the front door for them and followed them outside. As he gave the package to Ben, he said to Mandie, "Thank your grandmother for me for the order, young lady, and y'all do come back to see me again." Turning to Ben, he said, "Good day, Ben. I imagine you'd better hurry home. Mrs. Taft is probably waiting."

"Yes, sir," Ben agreed as the girls stepped up into the buggy.

As Ben drove away from the store, Mandie said, "Ben, Mr. Heyward was telling you in his own words not to take us anywhere else, wasn't he? Just straight back to Grandmother's?"

Ben cleared his throat and said, "Mistuh Heyward, he jes' be lookin' out fo' you young ladies' safety now dat thieves roam around town."

"I know," Mandie muttered. She wondered how they could ever get back to that alley again with everyone looking out for their safety.

When the girls got back to Mrs. Taft's house, Mrs. Manning was just driving up in her buggy. She stepped down and waited for the girls as Ben brought the vehicle to a stop at the front door.

"Hello, Mrs. Manning," Mandie greeted her as the three of them walked toward the front door.

"Nice to see you young ladies," Mrs. Manning said. Ella opened the front door, and they entered the hallway.

Mrs. Taft was coming down the corridor and stopped when she saw them. "Good morning, Mrs. Manning. Have you heard the news?" she asked.

Mrs. Manning frowned and asked, "What news, Mrs. Taft?"

"About the burglaries," Mrs. Taft told her as the two girls hung up their wraps.

"Oh dear, burglaries? Where?" Mrs. Manning asked as she and Mrs. Taft walked toward the parlor door.

The girls followed, Mandie carrying the package from Mr. Heyward's store.

"Right here in Asheville," Mrs. Taft explained as they sat down in the parlor. "Seems quite a lot of them have occurred without the authorities even knowing about it. And I have to tell you, my silver set that you wanted to borrow has been stolen."

"Stolen?" Mrs. Manning repeated, shocked. "How did that happen?"

Mrs. Taft explained about Uncle Ned's visit and the events of the day. Mandie and Celia waited quietly with the tablets.

"Nothing like that has ever occurred in this town before," Mrs. Manning said.

"Are you missing anything? Seems the thieves can get inside a house and back out with leaving any trace of how they accomplished this," Mrs. Taft said.

"I have not heard about this, and therefore I have not looked to see if anything is missing. But I certainly shall when I return home," Mrs. Manning said. "I'm so sorry about your silver set. That particular set was near and dear to your heart, wasn't it? I believe it was the one your mother gave you for your wedding present, if I remember correctly?"

"Yes, indeed, it was," Mrs. Taft said sadly. "It can't be replaced. If they had to take something, I wish they had taken something else. I do hope I will recover the set."

As Mandie listened to all this, she became more determined to find the burglars. She was going to get her grandmother's set back for her.

"I must be going," said Mrs. Manning. "I'll stop by Mrs. Chittendon's and ask if I might borrow her silver set for the church dinner. She has a large one like yours." She rose from her chair. "I sincerely hope you locate the set and that these men are brought to justice. In the meantime, I appreciate your warning me about these burglaries, and I will check my own belongings as soon as I get back to my house."

As soon as Mrs. Manning left, Mandie handed the package from Heyward's Store to her grandmother and said, "Are you ready to begin now, Grandmother?"

"Yes, of course, dear, and thank you for going for the tablets for me," Mrs. Taft said, accepting the package and removing the wrapping paper. "Now, if you and Celia want to help, let's put one of these tablets in each desk downstairs here so next time I can find one."

That was a bigger job than it sounded like. Mrs. Taft's house was very large, second in size only to Mr. Vanderbilt's mansion. The girls hurried around the many downstairs rooms, searching for desks and leaving a tablet in each drawer.

"Celia, I didn't realize that silver set was so important to my grandmother," Mandie remarked as they left the library room.

"I'd say it's one of her real treasures," Celia agreed.

"Yes, and I'm going to see that she gets it back. No crook is going to walk off with something that is so dear to my grandmother," Mandie declared.

Celia stopped to look at her. "Mandie, there is nothing we can do to find the silver set," she said. "Remember, these burglars may be dangerous, and we'd better not become involved in this."

Mandie's thoughts went back to Heyward's Store, where they had seen April Snow. That was something else she'd like to know. What was April Snow doing out and about by herself? The school didn't allow that. That girl had said she would make trouble for Mandie. What could she be plotting?

"Celia, I am going to find out what April Snow was doing in town by herself at Heyward's Store," Mandie remarked as they went down the hallway.

"But why, Mandie? She wasn't bothering us for a change," Celia said.

"No, but she is not supposed to go wandering around by herself. Miss Prudence wouldn't put up with that at all," Mandie replied. "Besides, she looked suspicious to me when she rushed out without saying a thing."

Celia stared at Mandie, her eyes wide.

"Don't look too surprised. Remember, April has been involved in certain kinds of things ever since we've known her," Mandie said. "I'll just check it all out, that's what I'll do."

Chapter 9 / Making Plans

The inventory took the whole day to complete. Mandie had not realized before how many valuable possessions her grandmother owned. Important papers and small items like jewelry were all stored away in safes. Mandie found that her grandmother had not just one but several safes in secret places throughout the house. Priceless vases and jade and crystal objects sat on shelves and tables in plain view for anyone to see. The paintings on the walls were originals and expensive.

"Grandmother, it must have taken you an awfully long time to collect all these things on your inventory," Mandie remarked. She and Celia were counting silverware in a plush case kept in the drawer of the buffet.

Mrs. Taft, making notations on her list, looked up at Mandie. "Oh dear, no, Amanda. It would take more than a lifetime to accumulate all that is in this house. You see, most of what I have was inherited from several lines of my family and also your grandfather's family."

Mandie paused with her hands full of silver spoons. "Well, then, Grandmother," she said, "why do you keep all this stuff? It sure is a lot of trouble to track down everything on your inventory list."

Mrs. Taft smiled at her granddaughter and explained, "You don't just give away the family's treasures that have all been dear to someone's heart. Why, it would be like giving away your memories." She bent over to write again.

"I sure am glad I don't own so much stuff like this," Mandie declared, continuing counting the spoons. And then she had a sudden thought and looked up to ask, "Grandmother, all this is from my mother's side of my family. Do you think Uncle John has these kinds of things that came down through his and my father's family?"

"Oh yes, of course he does. Why don't you ask him about it one day?" Mrs. Taft answered as she checked off items on her list.

"Oh no, Grandmother, I won't ask him. He might want me to help him with his inventory." Mandie laughed.

Mrs. Taft looked at her and laughed, too, then said, "Oh, he will definitely want you to help one of these days. After all, you will inherit everything from his family and also from your mother's family since you are the only heir. That is, unless your mother has another baby."

Mandie remembered her little baby brother who had died and her mother's health problems that had almost taken her from them, too. "Grandmother, I hope my mother never has another baby," Mandie said, her tone low and rather sad.

"I know you are thinking about what happened," Mrs. Taft said softly. "But, Amanda, women have babies every day, and it's not always like that."

Ella came to the dining room doorway and announced, "Miz Taft, supper is about to be ready. Where abouts you planning on eating it?" She looked around the room at the stacks of things that had been pulled out of drawers and cabinets and piled on the table for counting.

"Ella, let's use the breakfast room. It's just the girls and me, and Annie will eat with Mollie and Hilda in their sitting room again," Mrs. Taft instructed.

After Ella left, Mandie said, "Grandmother, we are finished with the silverware."

"Then that's the end of the inventory," Mrs. Taft replied. "Let's just stop and get washed up for supper now. We can put everything back in its place later. And I'm glad to say, the inventory accounted for everything. Nothing is missing except the silver set."

"But the silver set is very important to you, isn't it, Grandmother?" Mandie queried as she and Celia followed Mrs. Taft out of the dining room.

Mrs. Taft glanced back at her and said, "Yes, dear, very important. Let's just hope it turns up somewhere. Now, you two hurry up and get back down for supper."

"Yes, ma'am," both girls answered as they hurried toward the stairway.

Up in the room they were sharing, the girls con-

114

tinued their discussion of the thefts.

"Celia, I believe the thieves are connected with that alley somehow," Mandie said, quickly brushing her hair.

"They might be," Celia agreed. "I probably ought to change clothes." She inspected her dusty skirt.

"We don't have time, Celia. Besides, we don't look that dirty," Mandie told her over her shoulder.

"That's because our clothes are dark," Celia said, shaking her skirt.

Mandie shrugged. "Like I said, we look fine. Anyway, I sure hope Uncle Ned can find out who the thieves are." She put her hairbrush on the bureau. "I'd like to help catch them and get Grandmother's silver set back."

"Mandie, we have to leave all that to the law people," Celia argued again. "It's too dangerous for us to become involved."

Mandie smiled at her and said, "I didn't mean I'd like to capture the crooks. I'd like to help find out who they are so the sheriff could arrest them. I have a feeling they are hiding out in that alley."

"Just because Tommy and Robert said there are crooks in there," Celia reminded her, her tone doubtful.

"Not exactly," Mandie replied. "It's such an old, dilapidated place, it could be a refuge for such people." Walking over to the door, she added, "Come on. Grandmother is going to wonder what took us so long."

When they got downstairs to the parlor, Mrs. Taft was not there. Snowball was curled up on the hearth in front of the fire. He opened one eye to look up at his mistress and then went back to sleep.

"Maybe she has already gone to the breakfast room. Let's see," Mandie said.

As they walked down the long hallway, they saw Mrs. Taft standing at the back door, talking to Uncle Ned.

"Do come on in, Uncle Ned. You're just in time for supper. Did you put your horse up for the night?" Mrs. Taft was saying as the two girls approached.

"Ben did," Uncle Ned answered. "Yes, thank you for the invitation to supper." He moved into the hallway.

"Uncle Ned," Mandie greeted him. "I'm so glad you came back. Did you find out anything about the thieves?"

"Amanda, we will talk at the table," said Mrs. Taft, turning toward the breakfast room. "Let Uncle Ned get his breath first." She pushed open the door.

As they entered the room, Ella was adding another plate for the elderly Indian. Mrs. Taft motioned to everyone to sit down at the table.

After they all were seated, Mandie eagerly waited for the old man's news. However, she knew better than to start asking questions with her grandmother presiding over the meal. So she kept looking at Uncle Ned until finally he smiled and began his story of his activities that day.

While Ella poured the coffee, Uncle Ned said, "Not much found out today. Lots of burglaries all over town, but no one saw the thieves." He stopped to sip his coffee.

Mandie was bursting with questions but waited for him to continue.

"Does anyone have any clue yet as to what these people are doing with the things they are stealing?" Mrs. Taft asked. "Has anyone heard of any of the merchandise being offered for sale? They must be stealing it with plans to sell it in order to get the money out of it." Mrs. Taft passed the platter of ham to Uncle Ned.

The old man took a large piece of the meat, placed it on his plate, then passed the platter on to Mandie.

"No one heard a thing," he said. "Lawmen think maybe thieves take stuff to another town and sell it."

"Oh, I hope not. I'll never be able to recover my silver set if that's the case," Mrs. Taft told him, looking alarmed.

Mandie took a piece of ham and handed the dish to Celia. Mrs. Taft got the other dishes passing around the table, and the conversation lagged until everyone had finished filling their plates.

"We finished the inventory, and I'm glad to say, nothing else is missing," Mrs. Taft told him.

"Seems the thieves only took one thing from each house they entered," Uncle Ned said. "Most things silver. List put on front of courthouse, on depot door, and other places for people to see. Shows what missing and who belongs to."

"Has anyone offered a reward yet for their missing possessions?" Mrs. Taft asked.

"Yes, reward list with missing list," Uncle Ned told her.

"Then I'd better see about adding a reward for

the return of my silver set," Mrs. Taft said.

"Grandmother, could we go read these lists?" Mandie finally spoke.

"Maybe tomorrow, too late today," her grandmother replied.

Tomorrow would be Sunday, and Mandie could imagine everyone leaving church and going down to the depot to read the lists. Also, she and Celia would have to return to their school before curfew tomorrow night. Things were going too slowly. When was she going to get an opportunity to return to the alley? Celia probably wouldn't go with her for fear of getting into trouble. But that was all right, she'd just go by herself. She wasn't afraid— not very much, anyhow.

"Mandie, do you want another biscuit?" Celia asked, holding out the bread basket to her.

"Oh yes," Mandie said, quickly taking one and passing the bread on to Uncle Ned. "Uncle Ned, who has been helping you investigate the burglaries?"

"Cherokee kinpeople," he replied with a smile. "Come to town to help."

"But where are they? They haven't been here, have they?" Mandie asked.

"No, they stay in secret places, watch, wait," he explained.

"I wish there was something I could do to help," Mandie said, laying down her fork and sipping her coffee.

"Now, Amanda, there is nothing you can do, so please don't get any ideas of becoming involved in this. It could be very dangerous," Mrs. Taft quickly interjected, her voice firm.

"Yes, thieves dangerous people," Uncle Ned added.

"I understand," Mandie reluctantly agreed.

However, she was formulating her own plans. Tomorrow would be Sunday, and Tommy Patton would be there with his school class. Somehow she would get a chance to speak to him about the situation. She was sure she could interest him in helping investigate. He had always seemed very agreeable to her every wish.

After supper was over, the group went to the dining room and returned all the inventoried items back to their proper places. Uncle Ned helped with the ones belonging on high shelves. After that was finished, they all went back to sit by the fire in the parlor.

"Where are Hilda and Mollie, Grandmother?" Mandie asked after a break in the conversation between the adults.

"Annie is taking care of them," Mrs. Taft replied. "I told her to keep them within her sight every minute, so they are staying upstairs. I just can't have Mollie running all over town."

Mandie told Uncle Ned about Mollie climbing the tree and coming in through her window at school.

"Dangerous," he commented, shaking his head.

"Yes," Mrs. Taft agreed. "I will be sending Mollie back with Celia's aunt Rebecca on Friday. I can't have any peace wondering what she might be up to next."

"Are they going to church with us tomorrow?" Mandie asked.

"I really haven't decided about that yet," Mrs. Taft said. "I'd hate to keep them out of church, but I don't know if I can manage them."

"Mollie does not behave in church at home," Celia said. "Aunt Rebecca takes her to Sunday school and then leaves her in the playroom with some of the other children while she goes into the chapel for the preaching."

"I appreciate your telling me that, Celia. That's what I will do. I'll turn her and Hilda over to Miss Frompton for Sunday school and leave them with her," Mrs. Taft announced.

Mandie secretly wondered what would happen if Miss Frompton could not control Mollie.

At that moment there was a loud knock on the front door. Everyone paused to listen. Ella could be heard opening the door and greeting someone. "Yes, sir, come right in. I'll take your coat and hat. Miz Taft, she be in de parlor."

"Thank you, Ella," a male voice replied.

"Uncle John!" Mandie exclaimed. "Uncle John is here!"

Uncle John appeared at the door of the parlor as she stood up. He met her halfway across the room for a hug.

"Uncle John, I'm so glad you are here," Mandie said.

"Good evening, Mrs. Taft, Uncle Ned," John Shaw said. "Heard about the burglaries and came to see if I can help out in any way."

"Welcome, John. Come on over and sit by the fire," Mrs. Taft told him. "Have you had supper?"

"Yes, ma'am, I have," John Shaw told her as he took a seat nearby. Looking at Mandie, who had returned to her seat, he added, "In fact, I had the honor of dining with Miss Hope and the girls."

"You came by the school?" Mandie asked.

"Yes. I didn't know you were here, and I also wanted to be sure everything was all right at the school," he explained. "Everyone is safe and everything is locked up over there."

"Perhaps you'd like some coffee," Mrs. Taft suggested. "Amanda, would you please go ask Ella to bring us a coffee tray in here?"

"Yes, ma'am," Mandie said, getting up to leave the room.

"I'll go with you," Celia said, following her into the hallway.

Before they got to the kitchen, Celia put out a hand to stop Mandie. "I can tell you are planning something, Mandie," she whispered nervously.

"Planning something? I haven't said a word about planning anything," Mandie said with a frown.

"No, but I've been around you so long in so many escapades, I can practically read your mind," Celia told her. "And if you are thinking of going back to that alley, *please* don't do that. This is a very dangerous situation."

"Oh, Celia, you always dream up things," Mandie said, pushing past her toward the kitchen. "I haven't said anything like that tonight."

"Not tonight, but you are thinking about it. I can tell," Celia insisted, following Mandie into the kitchen.

Ella was busy putting dishes away in cupboards. She looked at the girls and asked, "Coffee, right? In de parlor?" She smiled.

"Right, Ella," Mandie said with an answering smile. "Everyone is getting to be a mind reader tonight, looks like."

"I'll have dat coffee in de parlor in two shakes of a sheep's tail," Ella said, taking a tray down from a shelf.

"Thank you, Ella," Mandie said, turning to leave the room. "Come on, Celia, let's go back."

As soon as the girls stepped back out into the hallway, Celia began again. "Evidently these thieves are from out of town," she said. "And they could be really dangerous. It's not worth getting mixed up in it, Mandie. You might end up in trouble—with the crooks, and with your grandmother."

Without a word, Mandie hurried back toward the parlor door. She knew Celia would hush as soon as they came within hearing of the adults.

"Ella will bring the coffee right in," Mandie told her grandmother as she sat back down. Celia joined her.

Mandie wondered how she would get around Celia. Her friend didn't want to be involved in the search for the silver set, so she would keep her plans secret. But how would she get away from Celia? She seemed to follow Mandie every minute, as good friends always do.

Also, how would she get a chance to speak to Tommy Patton at church tomorrow without someone overhearing the conversation? She had not decided exactly what she would say to Tommy, but she wanted to go back and search the alley. Maybe she would find the hiding place for all the loot the thieves were collecting. And she was a little afraid to go by herself. Now, if Tommy would agree to accompany her, she would feel secure.

Ella brought the coffee in, and Mrs. Taft served it. There were also sweet cakes on the tray, so Mandie helped herself to these.

"So you have not had any burglaries over in Franklin?" Mrs. Taft was asking John Shaw.

"No, not that we know of, but everyone in town has secured their houses because we are not that far away from here," John Shaw said, accepting a cup of coffee from Mrs. Taft.

Mandie remembered the inventory and told him, "Uncle John, you should see what all Grandmother has in this house. It took her and Celia and me all day to check it all out on her inventory list."

"And nothing is missing but the silver set," Mrs. Taft added. "I've come to the conclusion that it was stolen because it was sitting right out in plain view on the buffet and would have been quickly snatched. However, we haven't figured out how they got into the house in the first place."

"Some people in town say locks forced," Uncle Ned told her.

"We inspected all the locks, and nothing has been damaged," Mrs. Taft replied.

"There are so many ways a thief can enter a house," John Shaw said. "They've been known to even climb up on porch roofs and go in through windows, and come up through cellars."

Mrs. Taft shook her head. "We've checked it all out. No sign of entry anywhere."

As Mandie listened to the conversation, she was busily planning for her attendance at church tomorrow. Somehow she would get an opportunity to speak to Tommy Patton. Maybe she could bump into him on purpose when the service was over. But his class marched into church together and marched out together. It would be difficult to say anything to him without someone else overhearing it. She would figure it out before time to go to church tomorrow. She just had to ask him if he would go to the alley with her to search for her grandmother's silver set. And she really believed he would agree to this, if she could only have the chance to ask.

Chapter 10 / Fouled-Up Plans

By the next morning, the weather had turned much colder, and heavy rain drenched the town of Asheville. Mrs. Taft decided to leave Hilda and Mollie at home under the supervision of Annie while everyone else attended church.

Uncle John left with Uncle Ned after breakfast to continue the urgent search for the thieves and the stolen merchandise. Ben drove Mrs. Taft and the girls to church and stayed for the services himself.

They arrived early, and Mandie glanced around the churchyard to discover there was only one other buggy at the hitching post. "Grandmother, nobody is here yet," she commented as they stepped down from the rig. "We're awfully early."

"I know," Mrs. Taft said over her shoulder as she hurried for the door under the protection of her umbrella. "Let's get inside out of this rain."

125

The two girls, sharing an umbrella, rushed in the door behind her. Mandie had hoped Mr. Chadwick's pupils would have already arrived. She could then have walked right by them on the way to Mrs. Taft's pew. She had intended catching Tommy Patton's eye and mouthing a message to him. Now the boys would sit down near the back, and she, with her grandmother and Celia, would be sitting in their front pew as usual. She wouldn't have a chance to attract his attention.

"Come along, girls," Mrs. Taft said, looking back at them as they stood inside the door.

Celia immediately started up the aisle, and Mandie walked faster to catch up with her. She kept glancing over her shoulder, hoping the boys had arrived behind them. Several families came in, but there was no sign of the group of Chadwick students. She wished she were with her schoolmates because the girls sat together across the aisle from the boys, and she might have had a chance to attract Tommy's attention.

"Oh well," she murmured to herself as she followed her grandmother and Celia into the pew. She kept sneaking peeks back up the aisle when her grandmother wasn't looking. She knew Mrs. Taft would say that was very unladylike if she caught her.

Finally, Mandie heard the muffled commotion as the boys entered the sanctuary and tried to be quiet as they marched up the aisle to their seats. She glanced back in time to catch Tommy Patton's eye. She pretended to be touching her hat to straighten it when in fact she was trying to signal to him. He noticed and slowed down, causing Mr.

Chadwick to motion for him to stay in step.

"Let's talk," Mandie mouthed at Tommy.

Tommy paused again, but his classmates pushed him along into their customary pew. He sat down out of Mandie's view.

Maybe I can catch him on the way out, Mandie silently told herself. She couldn't see him now unless she turned completely around in her seat, and she knew better than to do that with Mrs. Taft present. She focused her attention on the song leader when he stepped forward and said, "Let's all stand and sing now, hymn number 193."

Hoping the people standing around her would not notice, Mandie again tried to signal with her fingers as she pretended to adjust her hat. However, this time she did attract the attention of her grandmother, who frowned at her and motioned for her to stop.

Joining in the singing, Mandie's clear voice could be heard above the others around her as the congregation sang, "How firm a foundation, ye saints of the Lord." The song leader looked directly at her and smiled.

When everyone was again seated and the minister had begun his sermon, Mandie's mind wandered. She knew the boys from Mr. Chadwick's school always stood and waited until all the other people had gone from the sanctuary before they left. Also, her grandmother always walked ahead of her toward the door. Maybe she could get Tommy's attention as she passed the boys' pew.

And this time she was lucky. As she walked out when the service was over, she was delighted to see that Tommy Patton was at the front of the line waiting to leave. Barely turning her head as she passed him, she casually moved closer and whispered, "Let's go to the alley," without daring to look straight at him.

Out of the corner of her eye, she saw him look at her in surprise, frown, then smile and whisper back, "All right."

There was no time for anything else as the people behind Mandie pushed forward and she had to quicken her steps.

Mrs. Taft looked up at the sky as they stepped outside and said, "I do believe it has stopped raining." Ben pulled the rig up near the front steps and helped Mrs. Taft up into it. The girls followed her, Celia first, and just as Mandie put her foot on the step to enter the vehicle, Tommy Patton appeared at her side.

"I believe you lost this," he said with a smile and held out her lacy handkerchief.

"Oh, I didn't realize I had," Mandie replied, glancing at her bag where the handkerchief usually hung from the strap. "Thank you."

"When?" Tommy whispered quickly.

"Tomorrow night, ten-thirty," Mandie whispered back. And then loudly added, "Thank you so much, Tommy, for finding my handkerchief," as she stepped into the rig.

"You're welcome," Tommy replied with a little wave as he turned away to join his classmates.

Mandie sighed in relief as she sat down. That was quite a coincidence. She had not lost her handkerchief on purpose. How convenient things had turned out. Celia had been close to her side, but Mandie didn't believe Celia would divulge her secret if she understood what had been going on.

The day passed without any further news from Uncle John or Uncle Ned. Mrs. Taft concluded they had not accomplished anything significant yet. And while Mrs. Taft was discussing this, Mandie kept thinking, *Will they look in the dark alley?* And if they did, what would they have found? More bums? Stolen merchandise? Or just plain nothing? She was awfully eager to go look for herself.

The day was still cloudy, and Mrs. Taft called the girls to her before suppertime.

"I think it best if you and Celia return to your school before dark," Mrs. Taft told them from her usual place in the parlor before the roaring fire.

Mandie was surprised. Mrs. Taft always had them stay for supper when they came to visit on Sunday. But this time she was delighted with the idea. She would get back to the school in time to talk with Miss Hope and some of the other pupils about the burglaries. They might have had some more news about this.

Ben drove them back to school with Snowball. Since the place had been securely locked up because of the trouble in town, he waited in the front driveway while Miss Hope came to unlock the front door and let the girls in. They waved good-bye as he drove away.

"I'm glad you girls came back before dark, what with all the trouble going on in town," Miss Hope said after greeting them. "I also appreciate your bringing Snowball back. I'll take him to the kitchen," she said as she took the white cat from Mandie.

Mandie and Celia had stopped in the foyer to

remove their coats and hats. Mandie asked Miss Hope, "Has there been any news yet? Uncle Ned came to Grandmother's and said he and his men were out hunting for these thieves."

"No, dear. We haven't heard a word from anyone," Miss Hope told her. "In fact, I was hoping you all would have some news. I do hope things get solved and everything settles down soon. It's such a strain on everyone here having to stay indoors."

At that moment Mandie caught a glimpse of April Snow darting around the corner of the hallway. She supposed the girl had been eavesdropping as usual.

"How is Miss Prudence?" Celia asked.

"She seems a little better, but she is still staying in her room in order not to spread any germs," Miss Hope replied. "She will probably be out and around in a couple of days."

"They have a list of the stolen things posted on the depot board, but we didn't get to go read it because of the weather today," Mandie told Miss Hope. "You don't have anything missing from the school here, do you?"

"No, dear, not that we have discovered, thank goodness," Miss Hope said. "And how is little Mollie?"

Mandie caught her breath, wondering if Miss Hope knew about the escapade up the tree. "I think Grandmother has decided she can't control her, so Mollie will be going back with Aunt Rebecca when she returns Friday. I sure would hate to have to take care of her. She is busy every minute, into something," Mandie said, shaking her head.

Miss Hope smiled and said, "I'm sure she will

outgrow all that as she gets older, especially with Celia's aunt teaching her. Now, you young ladies should get upstairs, unpacked, and ready for supper. And I'll take Snowball to the kitchen for his supper."

"Yes, ma'am," both girls agreed.

As Mandie and Celia started up the long, curved staircase, April Snow suddenly appeared and raced up ahead of them.

"Well!" Mandie exclaimed. "I suppose she listened to everything we had to say to Miss Hope."

"Which didn't amount to a hill of beans," Celia noted with a laugh.

In their room the girls quickly unpacked their overnight bags and changed into more comfortable dresses than their Sunday frocks. By that time they had to hurry downstairs to get in line for supper.

Most of the girls were fretting because they had been locked inside the school all day, not being allowed out because of the uncertainties.

"The thieves are stealing silver, not girls, so I don't know why we can't go outside," Thelma complained just ahead of Mandie and Celia in the line.

Thelma's friend Maybelle lowered her voice, "Oh, but I found a window that could be opened, the one at the back of the kitchen. All I had to do was unlatch it, and it's low enough I could step over the windowsill."

"You didn't!" Thelma exclaimed.

Maybelle put her finger to her lips and looked around quickly. "Yes, I did, and if you stay on the other side of the shrubbery bushes back there, no one in the house can see you," Maybelle explained in an excited whisper.

"Maybe I'll try it tomorrow if we are still locked in," said Clara Mae, the girl just ahead of the two.

Mandie quickly determined that would be the way she would slip outside tomorrow night instead of checking for the key to the back door. Miss Hope was keeping Snowball in the kitchen now, and she hoped someone else didn't go out that window and accidentally let him out.

The next night, after supper was over, Mandie and Celia went back to their rooms to curl up in the two big chairs with books.

When the curfew bell in the backyard rang at ten o'clock, Celia stretched to reach the pull string to turn off the electric light bulb in the ceiling, then went to the wardrobe to begin her preparations for bed. She stopped and looked at Mandie.

"Aren't you going to get ready for bed?" she asked Mandie, who had kept right on reading by the light of the oil lamp on the table.

"Not yet," Mandie said without looking up. "I want to read a little more." Celia shrugged and went back to the chair to pick up her own book again.

The girls silently read their books until twenty-five minutes after ten. Then Mandie glanced at Celia and silently rose from her chair. She went over to the wardrobe and got down her cloak and put it on.

Celia watched her, then asked, "What are you doing, Mandie?"

"Oh, I just thought I'd go back to have another look at that alley," Mandie said, nonchalantly pulling the hood up over her hair.

"Mandie, please don't go back to that place," Celia begged. "It could be awfully dangerous."

"I'm not afraid," Mandie assured her. "Besides, Tommy Patton is going to meet me at ten-thirty. Go on to bed. I'll be back soon." She started toward the door.

Celia instantly jumped up. "Well, if you are crazy enough to go back, I suppose I'll have to go with you," she said as she hurried to the wardrobe and took down her cloak.

"Celia, I just told you, Tommy is going with me," Mandie insisted.

"That's all right. I'm going, too," Celia replied.

Mandie sighed and said, "Well, come on, then. But please be very quiet. I'm going out through the window in the kitchen, and remember Snowball is in there and I don't want him following me."

"All right," Celia agreed.

Mandie quietly opened the door, walked down the hall, and carefully made her way down the staircase, with Celia following close behind. They slipped into the kitchen. Snowball, who had been asleep in the woodbox behind the cookstove, lifted his head to meow once but stayed where he was.

"Here," Mandie whispered, hurrying toward the window at the back. She reached for the latch and found it was not even locked. She pushed it up, and gathering up her long skirts, she sat on the windowsill and swung her feet over the edge to touch the ground.

Celia quietly followed her, and they both reached back to close the window.

"Where is Tommy going to meet you?" Celia whispered.

"He didn't say. Let's go around to the front," Mandie whispered back, leading the way through the shrubbery.

When the two came to the front yard beneath their room, three floors above, Mandie paused to look around through the darkness. There was no sign of Tommy. She walked a few paces in one direction, then the other.

"He isn't here," Mandie whispered.

"Let's get going, Mandie, before someone sees us. Tommy knows where the alley is," Celia urged.

"All right, let me get the lantern." Mandie hurried up the steps to the front porch and took down the lantern hanging by the door. She found matches in the tray beside it and returned to Celia without lighting the lantern.

The two girls hurried down the driveway to the road. The rain had left everything wet and muddy, and they tried to hold their skirts up.

"Keep a lookout for Tommy, just in case he does come," Mandie told her friend.

"He probably couldn't manage to get out of his school," Celia replied as they continued down the road.

Mandie's heart was pounding, and she silently wished Tommy had joined them. The night was cloudy and awfully dark. But she knew the way to the alley now and didn't light the lantern in order to not attract attention.

Once they came to the entrance to the alley, it was so utterly dark it was impossible to see into it. Pausing only long enough to strike a match and ignite the wick, Mandie led the way with the lantern giving out just enough light to see where they were stepping.

Celia whispered urgently, "Just where are you going in this alley, Mandie? What are you planning to do in here?"

"I don't know, Celia. Depends on whether we see anyone or not," Mandie answered.

"Well, I sure hope we don't see anyone," Celia replied. "Those crooks could be hiding out in here."

"That's exactly why I came back. They may have their loot stored up in one of these old buildings," Mandie said. She stopped for a minute. "Do you hear anything? Anyone?" she asked.

"No," Celia whispered in a shaky voice.

They came to one of the old, dilapidated warehouses, and Mandie held the lantern up to see the front of it. As she stepped forward, a large drainage grating in the road flipped up, and Mandie fell through, lantern and all.

"Help!" Mandie cried out as she landed below.

"Mandie, where are you?" Celia called frantically, circling around in the darkness.

"I'm under the road, Celia," came the muffled answer. "Help me figure out how to get out of here."

"Oh, Mandie, whatever are we going to do?" Celia cried, trying to locate where the voice was coming from.

"Walk around up there and see if you can find anyone to help me," Mandie called back.

"Find anyone? Oh, Mandie, but—" Celia began.

"Hurry up, Celia, look around. There may be someone up there," Mandie insisted urgently.

Mandie tried to light the lantern still in her hand, but she had lost the matches. As she groped around in the darkness, she kept bumping into things. She decided she was in a small compartment of some kind, and of all things was ankle deep in water.

"Mandie, it's so dark up here I can't see if there is anyone around," Celia called out. "Maybe I can find where you fell through and I can come down there."

"No, no, Celia, don't do that," Mandie exclaimed. "Stay up there where you can get help. If you come down here, nobody will ever see us to help us get out."

"Mandie, I'm so afraid, I don't know what to do," Celia wailed.

"There may be someone in one of those buildings up there. Go try the doors and see if any of them will open," Mandie urged her friend.

"I hope I don't run into that man who spit at us that day," Celia groaned as she pulled her cloak tight and peered anxiously through the darkness.

"Just ask anyone you see up there. Walk around, Celia, don't just stand there," Mandie told her. "Oh, why didn't Tommy Patton come with us?" she mourned under her breath.

Mandie was even more worried than Celia. She might not be able to get out of this place until daylight. And she would be in deep trouble at the school and also with her grandmother. She just had to get back up on the road somehow.

Chapter 11 / Trapped!

Mandie had no idea where she was, and she was afraid to move. She could imagine rats and snakes around her in the darkness. Damp and cold, she shivered all over. She clasped her cloak tightly around herself. Then she felt something in her pocket. She quickly reached inside, and sure enough, it was a match. Now, if she could strike it somewhere, maybe she could light the lantern.

"Celia, I found a match," she called up to her friend. She slid her hand over the lantern. It didn't feel wet. She would take a chance on striking the match on the metal base. Holding her breath, she ran the match across it. It flared! She quickly raised the shade a tiny bit and touched the lighted match to the wick. Her surroundings immediately glowed in the brightness.

"Mandie, did you get the lantern lit? I can see a light down there," she heard Celia call from above.

"Yes, Celia, and this seems to be some kind of tunnel I'm in," Mandie answered as she looked around. "I'm going to start walking and see if I can find a way out." She started to the right and came to a wall. Turning, she walked the opposite way, and as the light from the lantern shone ahead, she could see several openings in the walls.

"Which way are you going, Mandie?" Celia asked anxiously, peering over the edge of the opening.

"When you stand facing the building, I am going to your left. See if you can see any way out in that direction and yell down and let me know," Mandie instructed. "I'm moving on now."

Carefully sloshing through the ankle-deep water, Mandie finally came to an archway in the wall. Holding up the lantern, she saw it opened into a corridor. She saw several steps leading up into the opening. Quickly walking up to that level, she found she was at least in a dry passageway. Finally out of that murky wetness, she stomped her feet to try to get as much water as she could out of her shoes. She slowly made her way down the corridor toward a faint light ahead. She stopped to catch her breath.

"This must be the basement of one of the old warehouses," she murmured to herself. "I have no idea where I am going, but I have to go somewhere. So here goes," she decided. She moved slowly forward.

"There must be someone with a light in there," she noted when she saw that the light was coming from another room. "I don't think the light would be there by itself in this old place," she finished in a whisper.

As she came closer, she could see a broken window in the wall and a narrow door farther on. The light dimly illuminated stacks and stacks of merchandise of some kind in a large room. She cautiously crept toward the window for a better look. Her breath caught in her throat. A tall, lanky man in work clothes seemed to be writing on sheets of paper as he shuffled them on top of one of the boxes. The light was a lantern placed next to him on another box. Maybe he was running a business from there, she thought for a moment. But, no, everyone said there were no businesses in the old warehouses. So this must be some kind of illegal operation. But the room was filled with boxes. How could anyone have that much illegal merchandise?

Mandie suddenly realized she was at a dead end. As far as she could tell, she would have to go through that room to get out. Maybe if she put out the lantern, she could sneak between the tall stacks of boxes to the door on the other side of the room.

She was already shivering and shaking from her cold, wet shoes and skirts, and now fright added more to her trembling. Then she remembered she didn't have any more matches, and if she put out the lantern, how would she see her way beyond the room and out of this building? It was sure to be dark wherever that door led. Maybe she could shield the lantern light with her cloak as she slipped between the boxes. And she would have to be awfully quick and awfully quiet before the man saw her.

Mandie stared across the room at the open door on the far side. Suddenly she got a glimpse of Celia as she stooped behind a large box near it.

Gaining courage from knowing her friend was there, Mandie gathered up her wet skirts, shielded the lantern, and moved carefully through the nearby doorway. She tried to stay hidden behind the tall stacks of boxes as she crept into the room and headed toward the other door. She was nearly halfway across the room when the man turned and saw her. She stumbled in her wet skirts and, trying to hold on to the lantern, rushed for the far door. But the man was too quick.

"Whoa there," he said, grasping the back of her cloak and yanking her to a halt. "Now, just where did you come from?"

"I'm going home, mister. I'm lost," Mandie quickly replied, frantically trying to think of a satisfactory answer.

"I'll say you're lost," the man growled, still holding her cape.

Mandie glanced toward her friend, and Celia signaled that she was going for help. She quickly went back through the door.

"If you'll just let me go, mister, I have to go home now," Mandie told the man, trying to keep her voice from shaking in fear.

"You are not going anywhere right now till I find out how you got in here," the man insisted. He frowned as he bent to stare into her face.

"I . . . I . . . fell in, mister, I fell in," Mandie answered, trying to wrestle free from his grasp.

"Fell in, huh? That's just not possible, miss. No way you could have fallen in here," the man argued, gathering up more of her cloak in his hands. "Now, I don't want no nonsense. I am asking you one more time, how did you get in here?" He gave her a little shake with her cloak.

Mandie almost dropped the lantern in her fright. "There's—there's a hole up in the street, and I fell through it," she quavered. She took a deep breath and made herself look straight into his dark eyes.

He squinted at her and replied, "No hole up in the street. I know that. Now, tell me quick, how did you get in here?"

"I can show you," Mandie insisted, still staring into his face in order not to seem afraid. "It's in the street up there. I stepped on something. It flipped, and I fell through into a whole lot of water. Then I walked a long ways and found that window over there and this room." She pointed toward the window.

The man frowned, scratched his whiskers, and said, "You'd better tell me the truth. I'm going to keep you here until you do."

Then a familiar voice behind them said, "Nerlin Snow, you let her go! I told you I'd turn you all in if you don't straighten up and give back all the stuff you all have stolen."

Mandie turned her head and couldn't believe her eyes. April Snow was standing in the doorway.

"Oh, now, April, we just hadn't got around to it yet," the man whined, still holding on to Mandie's cape.

April walked across the room, slapped the man's hand, and forced him to let go of Mandie.

Whirling Mandie around by the shoulder to look at her, April said, "Now, you get on back to school. I can take care of him."

Mandie's thoughts whirled as she tried to figure out the situation. April had called the man Snow. "Thank you, April" was all she could think to say.

"Now, cousin, don't be so hasty in your actions," the man complained to April.

April whirled to face him. "Cousin, my foot. I don't claim kin with your kind. After all, you are only about a thirteenth cousin," she retorted, placing her hands on her hips. "Where are the rest of your friends?"

"They're not here right now," the man she called Nerlin Snow replied.

"I suppose they are out stealing more," April said. "You promised if I'd go buy those writing tablets for you to list what belongs to whom, you'd give everybody their stuff back."

"You know the law would grab us in a minute if we's dumb enough to do that," Nerlin said.

Mandie stood there listening, wondering what was going on.

April suddenly stomped her feet again and moved closer to Mandie. "I told you to go, get gone, hightail it. Get out of here. Understand?" she shouted.

Mandie stepped back. "Yes, I know you did, April, but I might ought to stay to help you. Maybe—"

"I don't need any help," April interrupted firmly.

Mandie glanced beyond April to the door behind her. Celia was standing there with Uncle Ned.

Tommy Patton hovered in the background. She breathed a huge sigh of relief.

April whirled again and saw the group in the doorway. "Come on in," she said. "This is one of the thieves who's been stealing all over town."

As Uncle Ned stepped into the room, Nerlin moved between two stacks of cartons. Tommy rushed in and went straight to Mandie. "I'm sorry," he apologized. "They had the school locked up, and I was late getting out. So I missed you."

"Thanks for coming anyway, Tommy," Mandie told him, trying to straighten her soggy skirt and cloak as she set the lantern on the floor.

Uncle Ned walked straight up to Nerlin where he was trying to hide between the boxes. "Why you steal?" he asked the man. "Big Book say do not steal." At least a foot taller, he stopped and stared down at the man.

"Oh, not one of them preacher kind of Indians!" Nerlin moaned, trying to stay out of Uncle Ned's reach.

"Nerlin Snow, you were raised by the Bible, just like I was," April jumped into the conversation. "You know it does say you should not steal, so don't get all ignorant all of a sudden." Then looking up at Uncle Ned, she said, "He is one of the thieves. There are two more that I know of. I warned him I would turn him in. He's not going to disgrace the name of Snow. But you all beat me to it. So tie him up, Uncle Ned, and just wait. The others will probably be in here before long. This is their meeting place."

Uncle Ned nodded down at April and said, "You a good girl."

Tommy came forward with a coil of rope and handed it to Uncle Ned. "Here, Uncle Ned, I'll help you tie him up, and then we can wait for the others."

For once in her life, Mandie was practically speechless. She thought of all the ill feelings she'd had toward April, and all the pranks April had pulled on her. And now here was an April Snow she had never seen before.

"Thank you, April," Mandie said again to the girl.

"Yes, many thanks, April," Celia finally spoke from the other side of the group.

April frowned at Mandie and said crossly, "Thanks for what? I haven't done anything to be thanked for. I just don't want any lawbreakers even slightly connected to my family name."

Uncle Ned and Tommy approached Nerlin, and since the man was backed into a corner, he finally just stood there and allowed the old man to tie his hands behind his back.

"That is not going to do you any good, you know," Nerlin said threateningly to Uncle Ned. "I have two friends who will be along shortly, and the odds will be against you then."

Uncle Ned did not reply but finished tying the man's hands.

Mandie had a sudden idea. She stepped up to the man and asked, "Now, tell me which box has my grandmother's silver set in it. I want to take it back to her. Right now." She stomped her foot and glared at him.

"How do I know where your grandma's stuff is? I didn't pack all these boxes," Nerlin said angrily.

"I want it right now," Mandie repeated, her voice firm.

"More'n likely it's done gone off on the train," Nerlin said offhandedly, spitting on the floor.

"On the train?" Mandie was shocked. "You'd better hope it hasn't, or you're going to be in deep trouble."

"When go on train?" Uncle Ned asked the man. "What went?"

"Several days ago we took some boxes to the depot," he grumbled. "They were supposed to be put on the train the next day," Nerlin replied. "So, you see, some of it is long gone."

"Where did it go on the train?" Mandie quickly asked.

"Who knows? I'm not the only one handling all this stuff, you know," Nerlin told her.

April stepped forward and stomped on the man's foot. "Stop lying, Nerlin," she said. "You didn't send anything off on the train. I've been watching. Now, where is Mrs. Taft's silver set? Tell her. Tell her *now*."

"How do I know what's in all these boxes?" Nerlin yelled back at her. "I didn't pack all of it."

"Then we unpack all the boxes," Uncle Ned told him. "We find it."

"Oh yes, Uncle Ned, let's do," Mandie quickly agreed.

April spoke again. "You'd better tie his feet. He'll run away."

"No run, tied to wall," the old Indian said.

Mandie walked around the man. The rope tying his hands was looped around several hooks on the wall behind him.

April glanced at the rope and nodded.

"Let's get all these boxes opened," Tommy said, pulling at the lid of one on the top of a stack.

Uncle Ned and Tommy lifted the boxes to the floor so Mandie and Celia could examine the contents. April crossed her arms and stood by the doorway, watching them.

The boxes contained all kinds of silver sets, silverware, jewelry, costly vases, and other expensive items. Pretty soon enough boxes had been emptied that there was hardly room to walk.

"Why don't we put some of this back in the boxes?" Mandie suggested, surveying the huge pile. "The only thing I want to find is Grandmother's silver set, and we know it's not in the boxes we've emptied."

"Yes, careful," Uncle Ned agreed, returning some of the items to a box he had searched.

"This might take all night," Tommy said with a big sigh. "Can't we make that fellow tell us which box Mrs. Taft's set is in?" He stared at the man.

"How many times do I have to tell you, I don't know what's in all those boxes. I didn't pack all of them," Nerlin retorted.

Uncle Ned straightened up and looked at Tommy. "Need search train," he said. "May be there."

"But, Uncle Ned, he said they took boxes to the train several days ago. Wouldn't it be gone by now?" Mandie asked.

"Train man promise lawman he hide, not put on train," the old Indian explained.

Mandie smiled and said, "Oh, I'm so glad. But are you going to search the train station tonight?"

Uncle Ned smiled. "Braves wait to search depot," he said.

"Oh, I just remembered, Uncle Ned," Mandie said quickly. "Where is my uncle John? He went off with you to help search."

"He search. See him soon," Uncle Ned told her, glancing at Nerlin, who was listening.

"So you haven't found my partners yet," Nerlin sneered. "Better hope they don't find you."

Mandie wondered where his partners really were. They might be dangerous. Uncle John could be harmed. As she thought about this, she quickly helped return the merchandise to boxes. But Uncle Ned's young braves were with Uncle John. He was bound to be safe wherever he was. She then looked at April Snow, still standing by the doorway. She knew she couldn't always trust the girl, and now she frowned as she reviewed the events of the night. April seemed to be honest about this, but could she really be trusted?

April, as though reading Mandie's thoughts, said, "I wouldn't lie about anything as serious as this, whether you believe me or not. And I don't really care what you think."

Uncle Ned, Tommy, Celia, and Mandie all straightened up to look at April. And just as they did, two burly strangers appeared in the doorway with guns at the ready.

The taller one spat on the floor and demanded, "What's going on here?"

No one said a word. They had all been caught unawares, even April. Mandie quickly glanced at Uncle Ned. He had laid his bow and arrow down in order to help with the boxes. Tommy stood there motionless with his fists clenched. Celia was holding on to a box to keep from collapsing in fright.

Nerlin finally broke the silence. "I told you they'd be along. You didn't believe me. I guess you do now."

April jumped in front of the two men, blocking their way into the room. "Put your guns away," she told them. "Your game is over."

The man who had first spoken quickly shoved April, causing her to fall to the floor. "Out of the way," he growled. "Ain't no game over till it's over."

He and his partner advanced into the room, both training their guns on the group. Mandie breathed hard to keep from fainting. She felt Celia clutch her hand and whisper, "Our verse."

"Yes," Mandie whispered back. Together she and Celia recited their favorite Bible verse, "What time I am afraid, I will put my trust in Thee." Mandie squeezed her eyes shut to concentrate. Suddenly she felt Celia give her hand a sharp tug.

Mandie opened her eyes and looked toward the two angry men. She saw what Celia was trying to signal her about. There in the doorway stood at least six young Cherokee braves with Uncle John.

At first the outlaws were unaware of the other men. Then Nerlin spotted them and yelled, "Behind you!"

As the two men swung around, the braves burst into the room and everything went wild. Mandie and Celia crouched together behind one of the large boxes. Tommy jumped into the fight with the men. They soon captured the two crooks.

"Oh, dear God, thank you," Mandie said fervently as she lost all her strength and sat down on the floor.

The next thing she knew, Uncle John was standing over her. "Amanda, I am shocked to find you here," he said, shaking his head.

Mandie attempted to straighten up and look at him, but she was unable to speak.

"Get up, Amanda. We are going to your grandmother's right now, and you, too, Celia," John Shaw firmly told the girls.

He held out a hand, and Mandie finally got to her feet. "But, Uncle John, we haven't found Grandmother's silver set yet."

"Let's go," her uncle said in a voice Mandie had never heard before. He seemed very angry with her.

All right, she would go with him. But she was still determined to find her grandmother's silver set, somehow, some place. She wouldn't stop until she found it.

Chapter 12 / Punished

Mandie and Celia followed John Shaw out of the old warehouse without speaking. They both knew they were in deep trouble. Mandie was surprised to see Ben waiting in Mrs. Taft's rig this time of night. As a matter of fact, she had no idea what time it was, but she knew her grandmother must have sent Ben with her uncle.

Everyone quietly got in the rig, and without a word, Ben shook the reins and headed for Mrs. Taft's house. Mandie closed her eyes and tried to think what she could possibly say to her grandmother to explain what had happened and why. By the time Ben pulled into the driveway of the great mansion, Mandie still had not figured out what to say.

When Ben brought the rig to a halt, the front door opened and Mandie saw her grandmother waiting inside the hallway.

"Thank you, Ben," John Shaw told him. "If you will wait a few minutes, I will be going back to that warehouse to finish things up. But first I must speak to Mrs. Taft."

"Yessir," Ben agreed and sat back in his seat.

The girls slowly followed John Shaw to the front door, and when they stepped into the lighted hallway, Mrs. Taft gasped in shock.

"Where on earth have you two been? Just look at you both!" Mrs. Taft exclaimed. "Straight up those steps, get bathed up and put on clean, dry clothing. I will be up shortly. Now, get a move on, both of you."

Mandie and Celia hurried up the stairs to the room they used when they visited Mrs. Taft. Both of them kept extra clothes in the wardrobe since they didn't have enough space in their room at school.

"I'm sorry, Celia, but we're in trouble," Mandie muttered as she quickly threw off her wet cloak and dirty clothes. She grabbed the first thing she found in the wardrobe to put on after bathing.

"I know, Mandie," Celia agreed soberly. She, too, removed all her apparel, though it wasn't as wet and dirty as Mandie's.

In just a few minutes the girls had cleaned up, and they sat down in chairs to wait for Mrs. Taft. Neither of them spoke. Mandie knew her punishment would be severe, especially with Uncle John relating all the events to her grandmother. She wondered how Uncle John had found them and why he had brought them here to Mrs. Taft instead of back to school. Someone must have missed them at school. She had thought they'd been able to leave through that window in the kitchen without being seen.

Then the door opened and Mrs. Taft came into the room. She walked around without speaking for a few moments and then sat down in a chair facing the two girls. Mandie held her breath. Celia looked miserable.

"Amanda, you know you are going to be severely punished for this mess you've been into," Mrs. Taft said.

"Yes, ma'am," Mandie replied in a low voice.

"And you, too, Celia, although I know Amanda well enough to realize this was all her planning," Mrs. Taft said, looking at Celia.

"Yes, ma'am, I'm sorry," Celia said meekly.

"Miss Hope has told me she cannot be responsible for you two any longer," Mrs. Taft continued. "Therefore, both of you will stay here with me, and Ben will drive you back and forth to school every day until you both learn to behave appropriately. There will be no side trips, no excuses, no participation in the school's social occasions, which also includes the Christmas celebration and festivities at your school."

Mandie inwardly groaned. She had hoped to have a part in the school play during the holiday season. Celia looked at her and shrugged.

"Now, Celia, since your mother is not immediately available to discuss this, I am acting on her behalf because of an agreement with her. When your aunt Rebecca comes after Mollie, I will have a talk with her. In the meantime, I am acting as your guardian. Is that understood?"

"Yes, ma'am, Mrs. Taft," Celia answered, her

voice low. She did not look up as she fidgeted with the ribbons on her dress.

"And speaking of your mother, Celia, she has just sent word that we are all invited to your home to celebrate New Year's Eve when 1903 comes in," Mrs. Taft continued.

Celia and Mandie both looked up at her without speaking.

"But as part of Amanda's punishment, she will not be allowed to go," Mrs. Taft continued. "And after your uncle John reports to your mother, Amanda, we will see what else will be added to your punishment." She stood up quickly and said, "Now, get ready for bed and don't leave this room until time for breakfast, which is only about three hours from now. However, I will expect you both up, dressed, and ready to be at the table at seven o'clock sharp, after which Ben will drive you to school." She started toward the door and turned to say sharply, "Good night, both of you." She left the room.

"Good night, Grandmother, I'm sorry," Mandie said hurriedly as Mrs. Taft closed the door. "Celia, I'm sorry I got you mixed up in this, and if you don't want to be friends with me any longer I'll understand."

"Mandie!" Celia exclaimed. "What are you saying? I do things on my own decision. It's not your fault at all. And if you don't want to be my friend anymore, why, I'll . . . I'll just change to another school somewhere else."

"No, Celia!" Mandie said, quickly rising to reach over and squeeze Celia's hand.

Celia smiled at her and said, "All right then,

that's the last we will ever say about that."

"Agreed, and we had better get to bed," Mandie replied, going to the huge wardrobe to get out nightclothes.

"I just hope I wake up in time," Celia said, hurrying to get her own things.

"Don't worry. I'll be up on time because I probably won't sleep a wink," Mandie told her.

But Mandie did go to sleep. All too soon, Ella, the maid, came to wake them. "Time to rise and shine," she said, shaking both the girls.

Mandie slowly sat up in bed, rubbed her eyes, and said over a yawn, "Oh, how can I go to school half asleep?" She swung her legs over the side of the bed.

Celia slid off on her side and stretched. "I'll probably go to sleep in class," she complained.

"Better get dressed now and hurry downstairs," Ella told them. "That Mr. John, he be waiting for y'all."

"What a day this is going to be," Mandie moaned as she rushed to get her clothes out of the wardrobe.

The girls got dressed and rushed downstairs, where they found Mrs. Taft and John Shaw sitting by the fire in the parlor. All the girls dared say was "Good morning." And there was no discussion about the events of the night before. Mandie was dying to know what happened after they left the warehouse but did not dare ask.

Ella soon announced that breakfast was ready, and everyone filed out on the way to the breakfast room. Uncle Ned came in the front door and silently signaled to Mandie without the others seeing him.

"I'll be right there," Mandie whispered to Celia and quickly turned back.

Celia nodded and followed the adults on down the hallway.

When Mandie got back to Uncle Ned, he silently opened the front door and pointed to a box on the porch. Not understanding, she looked at him and bent to see what was inside the carton.

"Grandmother's silver set!" she exclaimed excitedly. "You found it!"

Uncle Ned smiled at her and said, "You take to Grandma."

"Oh, thank you, Uncle Ned, thank you," she replied, reaching to squeeze his hand.

He picked up the box and gave it to her. It was heavy, but she could manage it. "Come on, Uncle Ned," she told him and led the way down the hallway to the breakfast room door.

She went to Mrs. Taft and set the box down on the floor. "For you, Grandmother," she said, stepping back to watch as her grandmother bent to examine the contents.

"Oh dear, my silver set!" Mrs. Taft exclaimed and beckoned to Mandie to come nearer. She reached and hugged Mandie tight and said, "Thank you, dear, thank you."

Mandie put her arms around her grandmother and was so overcome she could not speak. She quickly went to sit by Celia.

Mrs. Taft greeted Uncle Ned, and he sat down at the end with the adults. Mandie and Celia ate silently while the situation of the night before was being discussed.

"So April Snow turned out to be not all bad after all," Mrs. Taft said after she had been told about the girl's appearance at the old warehouse.

"I have never believed anyone is all bad. There's bound to be something good about everyone, I think," John Shaw said. "It just takes some doings to find it sometimes."

"I will be speaking to Miss Hope on behalf of April," Mrs. Taft said. "I'm hoping the girl won't be expelled."

Finally, Mandie got the courage to speak. "If it hadn't been for April suddenly coming into that room, I don't know what that bad man would have done. He wouldn't believe anything I said."

"Just let that be a lesson, Amanda," Uncle John said. "You have to quit getting yourself involved in dangerous situations. One of these days there may not be anyone to get you out."

Mandie shivered and answered meekly, "Yes, sir." Looking around the table, she said, "I love you all. I really do. And I try to behave, but sometimes I just get carried away. I've been thinking and trying to figure out why this happens to me. But please don't ever forget, no matter what I do, I love you all dearly." Her blue eyes filled with tears. She dabbed at them with her white linen napkin.

"And we certainly all love you, Amanda, and Celia, also," Mrs. Taft said, laying down her fork. "That is why we get so upset when you get into all these dangerous escapades. If we didn't love you, we wouldn't care. Do you and Celia understand that?"

Mandie nodded and managed to say, "Yes, ma'am."

"Yes, ma'am," Celia added in a quiet voice.

"Now, let's get this meal finished. You two young ladies have to go to school today, you know," Mrs. Taft reminded them. "And please don't discuss anything with the other girls at school, mainly for April's sake. The less said the better. Miss Hope already knows the whole story, and I suppose she will relate the events to Miss Prudence. And when Miss Prudence gets well enough to leave her room again, I don't believe she will even mention this matter. Miss Hope has promised. So consider the matter closed and remember to behave yourself in the future."

Mandie nodded and said, "Yes, ma'am, Grandmother."

Celia added, "Yes, ma'am, Mrs. Taft."

"Now that we have all that settled, you girls hurry up and finish your meal," Uncle John said with a little smile. "I'll go with you all out to the barn for Ben to harness up the rig."

Mandie wondered why they should all be going to the barn when Ben always brought the rig to the front door for them. But she didn't think she'd better question Uncle John, so she remained silent and just looked at Celia with raised eyebrows.

As soon as the meal was finished, Mrs. Taft told them to get their coats. Their cloaks had been left hanging outside the wardrobe to dry, but they both had extra coats, which they put on.

"I don't understand why Uncle John wants us to go to the barn for Ben to harness up the rig," Mandie mumbled to herself as she hastily found a hat and gloves.

"Maybe Ben has something to tell us that we don't know about yet," Celia suggested.

Mandie shrugged. "I can't imagine what that would be. The thieves have all been caught, and the merchandise is all found. It's being returned to the owners, according to the conversation at the table just now."

"Well, come on, let's go find out," Celia said, heading toward the door.

Mandie stopped suddenly. "Oh, Celia, I forgot all about Snowball. I hope he's all right, and that someone didn't let him out."

Celia laughed. "If they did, he always finds you. So don't worry about it. Besides, Miss Hope is looking out for him. Come on."

Mrs. Taft was waiting downstairs, and Mandie was surprised to see that she had put on her coat, too. *Oh, goodness, that must mean she is going to school with us. Oh no!* Mandie's heart sank.

"Come on, girls," Mrs. Taft said as Uncle John opened the back door.

Mandie looked around and didn't see Uncle Ned. Had he left without saying good-bye? He never did that.

"Let's go, girls," Uncle John urged them.

Mandie and Celia quickly followed Mrs. Taft out into the yard. She stopped and allowed Uncle John to go ahead.

Mandie could see Ben standing by the door to the barn, but there was no sign of Uncle Ned. She and Celia followed Uncle John to the barn door.

"Good morning, Ben," Mandie greeted Mrs. Taft's driver.

"Mawnin', missies," Ben replied with a big grin. "Great day today!"

Mandie frowned and looked up at the cloudy sky full of rain clouds. A great day indeed? Looked like more rain today, and it was also colder. She shivered slightly.

"Come on inside, girls," Uncle John said, leading the way.

The moment Mandie stepped inside, she heard whining and squealing back in a corner. She rushed to investigate. There was a mixed brown mother dog and about half a dozen puppies.

Mandie laughed with delight as she stooped to pet them. "Oh, Uncle John!" was all she could say. She wondered if the dogs might have come from the old warehouse, but she didn't know if she should ask.

"Yes, Amanda, you did hear a puppy the time Ben brought you and Celia through the alley and the rig broke down. Uncle Ned found them last night," John Shaw explained.

Mandie suddenly realized the old Indian was standing nearby watching. She jumped up and ran to hug him. "Oh, Uncle Ned, thank you for saving them. Thank you."

"No home no more so bring them to Grandma," Uncle Ned said with a big grin. He looked at Mrs. Taft and added, "She say we keep awhile."

"Grandmother, thank you," Mandie rushed over to embrace her.

"Hold on, now, Amanda," Mrs. Taft said, laughing herself. "We are not keeping all these puppies forever, just until they can be weaned from the mother. Then we'll talk about whether you may keep one for yourself—that is, if you have obeyed and stayed far away from trouble."

"I promise I will, Grandmother," Mandie said excitedly.

"Think before act, Papoose," Uncle Ned reminded her.

"I always try to remember to do that, but sometimes things happen so fast I forget," Mandie said sadly.

"Remember to use thinking cap," the old Indian told her.

"All right, girls, you don't want to be late for school," Mrs. Taft reminded them. "Get outside now so Ben can harness the rig."

As soon as the rig was ready, Mandie and Celia climbed aboard. Mandie looked back and waved as Ben drove it down the driveway.

She did a lot of thinking on the way to school. She knew she had been willful and disobedient, and she tried to figure out how she could overcome that fault. If she could just remember to think first and then act, as Uncle Ned kept telling her, she wouldn't get herself and others in so much trouble.

Looking outside at the dark sky as they rode along, she murmured quietly, "I'm sorry, dear God, for doing what I knew was wrong. Please help me to be better, please. I thank you." She turned to look at her friend, who seemed to be doing the same thing. Reaching across the seat, she squeezed Celia's hand and said, "I'll try to grow up and be good and be a young lady."